# A HARDER THING
# THAN TRIUMPH

## Written by Barbara Ninde Byfield

A HARDER THING THAN TRIUMPH
FOREVER WILT THOU DIE
SOLEMN HIGH MURDER (WITH FRANK L. TEDESCHI)

SMEDLEY HOOVER: HIS DAY (WITH SARA KRULWICH)
THE BOOK OF WEIRD (ORIGINAL TITLE: THE GLASS HARMONICA)
THE EATING IN BED COOKBOOK

ANDREW AND THE ALCHEMIST
THE HAUNTED TOWER
THE HAUNTED GHOST
THE HAUNTED CHURCHBELL
THE HAUNTED SPY

## Illustrated by Barbara Ninde Byfield

TALES OF TERROR AND MYSTERY BY SIR ARTHUR CONAN DOYLE
HADASSAH: ESTHER THE ORPHAN QUEEN BY WILLIAM H.
    ARMSTRONG
THE CABLE CAR AND THE DRAGON BY HERB CAEN
TV THOMPSON BY GLENDON AND KATHRYN SWARTHOUT
THE MYSTERY OF THE SPANISH SILVER MINE BY HARVEY SWADOS
THE GIANT SANDWICH BY SETH M. AGNEW
UPRIGHT HILDA BY DONALD HUTTER

# A HARDER THING
# THAN TRIUMPH

BARBARA NINDE BYFIELD

PUBLISHED FOR THE CRIME CLUB BY
DOUBLEDAY & COMPANY, INC.
GARDEN CITY, NEW YORK
1977

"To a Friend Whose Work Has Come to Nothing" by William Butler
Yeats is reprinted by permission of Macmillan Publishing Company, Inc.,
M. B. Yeats, Miss Anne Yeats, and The Macmillan Company of London
and Basingstoke from *The Collected Poems of W. B. Yeats*. Copyright 1916
by Macmillan Publishing Company, Inc., renewed 1944 by Bertha Georgie
Yeats.

Library of Congress Cataloging in Publication Data

Byfield, Barbara Ninde.
A harder thing than triumph.

I. Title.
PZ4.B9936Haz [PS3552.Y65]    813'.5'4
Library of Congress Catalog Card Number 76–50709
ISBN: 0-385-12658-1

For
Jeanette and Curtis Roosevelt
The Best of Friends

Now all the truth is out,
Be secret and take defeat
From any brazen throat,
For how can you compete,
Being honour bred, with one
Who, were it proved he lies,
Were neither shamed in his own
Nor in his neighbors' eyes?
Bred to a harder thing
Than Triumph, turn away
And like a laughing string
Whereon mad fingers play
Amid a place of stone,
Be secret and exult,
Because of all things known
That is most difficult.

W. B. Yeats

*To a Friend Whose Work Has Come to Nothing*

# A HARDER THING
# THAN TRIUMPH

# GENESIS: *Louisa and Channing Adaams.*

Channing Adaams finished checking the labels his secretary had attached to the shipping cartons stacked on the floor of his office at the Bayard Foundation. "Very good, Miss Wilber. If you'll just see the two that stay here are taped, that'll do to keep the dust out. What you must do is be sure the mail room tapes *and* ropes the others. Especially the ones for Greenfield College. I don't know what their handling facilities are, and those books are heavy. And of course the books and files for Beemeadows may very well be delivered by covered wagon."

"Oh, Mr. Adaams," she giggled, "your farm can't be that rustic!"

"We often wish it were. Now, nothing is to be shipped until the first of April when we're back from this last tour. I suppose if the mail room here gets short of space it could all go to Adaams Park—you've made sure it can all be held here?"

"Oh, yes, I reserved the space myself. They'll have a corner all to themselves." Adaams almost expected her to reassure him she would water and feed the cartons once a week.

"Good. Now, what else?" He glanced out the window at the wet, thick snow falling, pulled a watch on an antique chain from his breast pocket. "Mrs. Adaams should be downstairs now; I hope this snow isn't going to delay our flight. Well, Miss Wilber, I'm off. You have my itinerary if anything comes up, but I trust you to get Mortimer off on the right foot and make him cope. From now on I'm only a very part-time consultant for the foundation, even on this last trip. You've always run the Bayard anyway; just don't let my successor find out!"

He gave her a rare, winning smile, patted her shoulder, and left the splendid glass cage that had been his office as president for the last twelve years. Mortimer's now; when Channing came back occasionally—and he'd be sure to see it was only occasionally—the consultant's fee the foundation had settled on when he'd resigned didn't entitle them to much more—he'd have a cubby somewhere downstairs. Miss Wilber would see to it that it wasn't too far from the center of things.

He hurried down the carpeted hall, smoothing his thick, springy, leonine hair, and into the elevator one of the stenographers was holding for him. No more perks like these again, he thought, as he climbed into the foundation's limousine where Louisa was waiting with their luggage. The driver swung out into the midtown traffic and headed down Second Avenue for the tunnel and Kennedy Airport.

"All finished, dear?" Louisa, anticipating the hot weeks ahead in Africa, was belted into her thin gray spring raincoat and had turned the heat up in the back of the car. Her coat and the car's upholstery matched a handsome streak that had recently begun to show in her abundant dark hair.

"All finished. Miss Wilber, by the way, was almost in tears over the little clock—and your note."

"Channing, I do hope you copied it in your own writing?"

"Oh, yes. 'For Grace Wilber: One hour for each year of service and support.' Very elegantly put, Louisa."

"I'm glad she liked it. The clock was a good choice for you to give her, no implication of 'the office wife' or any of that. I'll try to find something a bit more exotic to bring her from Africa from both of us; I've just seen your agenda and you won't have a minute, will you?"

"As usual. Hard to believe this is the last trip, isn't it?"

"I daren't, until we're back. And at the farm. Unpacked For good."

"If I didn't need your Spanish and Portuguese this round you'd be there now." Channing was rearranging papers in his briefcase. Louisa looked out at the snow, flipped on a reading light for him as the heavy car seemed to pour itself into the sooty damp gloom of the tunnel.

"No, I'm glad I'm going with you this last time. Not just to translate, although I imagine we'll find it very depressing, but because when we do finally move to the farm I don't want to do it alone. I want you to carry me over the threshold."

"Literally?" His eyes twinkled over the rim of his glasses.

"Literally. Here we are, fifty years old, and every place I've ever lived, and the both of us together, has been someone else's. The farm is ours. Over the threshold. Promise?"

He laughed, patted her hand, closed his briefcase. "I promise." He took off his glasses, closed his eyes, smiling.

Louisa smiled inwardly. All her life she had felt a bit like Mrs. Burton, receiving instructional telegrams from her peripatetic husband, succinctly commanding her to "Pay, Pack, and Follow." First with her widowed father, a career State Department official, with short ministries to the more comfortable countries and, later, longer embassies in the mud and mosquito posts—especially during the war, in South America. She had married Channing in 1942 just as he entered the Navy, had wanted to wait in Boston for what leaves he could get from the Altantic Fleet, but he had urged her to continue running her widowed father's household until the war was over. Anstruther, a distant cousin in the far-reaching Adaams family, was clearly running through his personal fortune in maintaining his ambassadorial style. Louisa, his only child, could not only keep an eye on that end of things and hold down the old man's flamboyance a bit, but spin straw into gold for Channing by solidifying acquaintanceship, and where possible friendship, with the powerful and influential who passed through her father's life. Far more useful to Channing's future than rolling bandages in Boston.

Channing had been right, of course, she mused; by the time her father died there was little to leave her, in spite of her economies, except a nonworking farm of 175 acres in the Berkshires, with a house and outbuildings all in need of repair. Beemeadows Farm. But by then Channing had used his leaves in London well, was on his way. Still in uniform, he had been present at the historic sessions of the United Nations at Church House in London in 1945, Louisa joining him, returning with him to the newborn Secretariat the next year where he worked closely with Eleanor Roosevelt, Tom Connally, all the others who, from time to time, had been wartime guests at Ambassador Anstruther's table. They had not forgotten his daughter's gracious and impeccable hospitality, they nodded with approval at her alliance with the prestigious Adaams family now that Channing was back from the war.

Remembering his brilliance, energy, thrusting efficiency, the benign and beneficent blind spot in his nature that did not allow him to see failure as a possibility, she knew that Channing would have achieved all he had without her, and without the Adaams name with its implications of generations of accomplished, distinguished ancestors. But, seeing him dozing in the corner as they came out of the tunnel, it had helped, being an Adaams, and she had helped. He had, quite simply, gotten there quicker.

In 1950 they had left the *ménage à trois* Louisa had somehow survived with Channing's mother in her house on Washington Square. Channing had been directed to head new peace-keeping operations and an information center in Central America for the United Nations; at thirty Louisa felt herself beginning to come into her own, at least in terms of services she could provide for Channing; her own hospitality, of course, instead of Marguerite's, but some of the South

American Indian dialects she had kept herself busy with learning during the war proved useful as well in a sticky situation or two. Channing had more than once left her behind in some forsaken outpost to sort out and translate agreements with local officials while he himself returned to headquarters to begin other negotiations.

Back to New York in 1957 after seven years of success, Channing had found a new regime, and one which was clearly a dead end for him, at the United Nations. New England, Boston, beckoned; born during and of the New Deal, Paul Revere College needed new blood, new blood but with a distinct tinge of blue and overtones of ancient ivy, the reassurance to the first graduating class of '36 that only a Cabot, Lowell, Roosevelt, Adaams could provide. The board of trustees had to offer a bit of retrospective éclat to the millionaire graduates they were now approaching for contributions to the endowment fund.

Again, Louisa ran a restaurant, a hotel, a conference center from the vast, high-hipped, and inconveniently renovated president's house on the campus. Channing began to be in demand for lectures, farther and farther away; instead of decreasing demands on her time, he brought and sent into the college's circle more and more guests from his increasing circle of colleagues. Well, Louisa reflected, a lot of it had been fun, in spite of the wallpaper and those dreadful chandeliers. And heaven knew the lectures paid, extraordinarily well. They were able to begin a small investment portfolio, keep the roofs at Beemeadows in repair, begin to rent it during the summer and have occasional fall and spring weekends there themselves.

Channing's mother, the formidable Marguerite Pittston Adaams, had long ago given up Washington Square and, quite against all the provisions governing the use of Adaams Park, had moved herself into a rambling suite in the great family estate on the Housatonic, blithely ignoring the thickets of legal barbed wire old Schuyler Adaams had strung out generations before to ensure that Adaams Park be maintained and administered as a library, museum, and conference center. He had wisely foreseen it would be too expensive for any one branch of the family to maintain as a residence; certain definite tax advantages for the trusts he had set up had been achieved in establishing "museum" status for it. Thus, the public was grudgingly let in three days a week—by appointment only, reservations four months ahead. If a certain preference was still given to applicants with indisputably WASP names, no one had yet made a fuss.

Visits to Adaams Park, to Marguerite, were pleasant enough; Channing, of course, did use the library and staff ruthlessly for his lecture material. Louisa rather enjoyed a day or two of being a passenger instead of an engine as she watched the staff cope with the guests, the furnace, kitchen, gardens, the mechanics of it all. Toward the end, it had become difficult and then impossible; Marguerite became angrier and ruder each visit about her lack of a grandchild. Channing had finally forbidden Louisa to see her at all, leaving her in Boston when he had to visit the Park himself.

Poor Marguerite, Louisa reflected, her last years of intermittent senility, dropsy, three shifts of nurses for years. Well, that was all over now; Marguerite was buried with the rest of the family years ago, the paucity of her estate—except for her jewels, which she had worn to the last—perhaps explaining those last years, free, at Adaams Park.

It had begun about then in their minds, in their forties, the idea of Beemeadows Farm as a community for those who Channing saw, far ahead of his time as was his gift, would be at the mercy of earlier and earlier retirement, compulsory or optional, still young enough and with enough resilience to begin an entirely new life rather than simply declining into less and less of the old life. An idea, but one that seemed to grow, stick like a comfortable burr, throb, begin to be a very real part of their plans.

Again to New York, in the late sixties—'67, it was, she recalled. Channing left his eight years at Paul Revere illuminated by an innovative and highly publicized exchange program with four other neighboring colleges, a successful endowment drive, and a flourishing and much envied Latin American summer studies program. The Bayard Foundation, its hushed, deep-piled floors in the East Side glass skyscraper, spread its golden beneficence over the developing world. Channing, as president, was its eye and ear, the Three Fates in one, here and there around the world, deciding if these wells would be dug, that road or dam built, this hospital funded, that school, technical institute enlarged. Ostensibly the job demanded perhaps three one-month trips a year; Channing saw more scope for the foundation, extended the traveling, continued his lectures on the uses and misuses of political power in increasingly greater circles.

One of old Marguerite's last bits of Machiavellianism was to have Channing elected to the board of the creaky, antiquarian Teaparty Trust in Boston; there had always been an Adaams on the board and Channing's cousin, Perceval Giffard, was hoping for the nod. How he would have loved it, too, and given much more to it than the token presence and name that was all the trust expected. And could have used the twenty-five hundred a year the directorship paid. But Marguerite had danced the Lancers years ago with more than one director; her son was chosen as chief executive officer almost automatically, with little to do aside from monthly meetings of the board, the trust being run with quiet efficiency by the executive director, a full-time professional with contacts as passionate as his own in seeing that as little as possible ever changed in Boston.

That stipend, however, saw to it that as much as possible

was beginning to be changed at Beemeadows: roofing, plumbing, insulation, fences. They were aiming at a goal now. Louisa, bred to thrift from her New England cradle, cut corners where they would not pay off, made do with Marguerite's old curtains and carpeting from Washington Square, saw to it that the New York apartment they chose would produce the most mileage in the entertaining Channing's job made necessary but cost them the least possible in behind-the-scenes amenities. Someday her life would include enough closets; she was content to wait.

Surprisingly, they had found from the beginning—when Channing was at home and had time to pursue it—a number of friends interested in one degree or another in the idea of Beemeadows Farm. Perhaps not really surprisingly; they were all of an age now to have seen their parents' last years, the nursing homes, the friction that wore away love and memory if there weren't nursing homes, the obligatory gray Sunday afternoon visits if there were. The life-support machines eating away thousands of dollars in hopeless, mindless vegetation. If it were only fear that drew their minds to an alternative at Beemeadows that might be enough to make it work. But Channing hoped, and Louisa knew how very much, that even if it were fear that brought them together it would be companionship that kept them there. How he would have loved to be the father of a large family, organizing, running, directing the whole thing. Well, no point in thinking of that. They'd faced that one years ago when they came back from Central America—Channing before Louisa, not letting her even know he'd been tested until his sterility was definitely established. Mumps. How stupid. Dear man, he'd wanted to save her the infinitely more discommoding poking and prying and temperature-taking that would have been necessary for her.

Ray Russell, Channing's investment adviser, had done well with the scraps and pieces he'd been given to work with, much of it from a sale of Marguerite's jewelry, although Channing had insisted on keeping a few pieces for sentiment. The income from their portfolio now, plus the Teaparty Trust, and Channing's "part-time" work—Louisa smiled to herself at Channing ever doing anything part-time—made it all possible; suddenly, after over a decade at the foundation, the increasingly intense dreaming was no longer a dream. Colonel Alfred Bemis, U.S.A., Ret., had already bought in, winterized the little log cabin on the edge of Beemeadows' 175 acres, and was there now, a hale and hearty fifty-three and amazed at how far his army pension went if one lived simply in the Berkshires. The Scotts, who for a few more years intended to be away off and on finishing an anthropological dig, were in the main house until spring, when they would begin building their own small house by the orchard. And Perce would join them from Adaams Park when Louisa and Channing were back, but not until late May when the weather was better.

Channing opened his eyes, yawned. "Talk to Perce this morning?"

"I was just thinking of him. Yes, just before I left. I know he isn't quite looking forward to leaving the Park after all these years, but he sounded cheerful enough. Poor dear, he's been there well over forty years, since college. It must be a dreadful wrench."

"All the more reason for our doing it ourselves now, when we're not besotted and beholden to any institution or way of life. Don't worry about Perce; his successor's already there and he'll have a few last glorious months breaking the poor chap in."

"Channing, do you think he'll be really happy in the community? He's such a—well, celibate, you can't count those three years with Terry, they were so long ago—I'm worried that the necessary gregariousness that's got to be part of the life will be hard for him. Not that we've laid it on too thick, but we all do agree that there has to be some obligatory contact, if only communal dinner, if it's going to work. Perce has gotten more and more into being a hermit. And he *is* so much older than the rest of us, you know."

"Louisa dear, what we must do is see that Perce is a cenobite, not an anchorite. That'll suffice. Left alone, but attached both physically and socially. Not off by himself up in one of the meadows. That's precisely why I assigned him half the old chicken house to renovate, not just for economy's sake. It's physically close to the main house where we'll have dinner, he'll have a neighbor in the other half one day soon I hope, and by force of sheer geography he'll be running into people."

"I see. Not exactly a communal decision, was that?" She twitted him gently. "But very shrewd, Channing."

"You'll come to see, my dear, that there will be times when communal decision-making has to be suspended when someone has a better idea."

And, thought Louisa, that someone will usually be you. After a lifetime of making things happen because of you, where most people let things happen to them, can you manage all of a sudden not to run things? I know the last thing you say you want at Beemeadows is to run it, but—is it only another hobby, like the stamps, butterflies, photography, all those—well, perhaps it'll solve itself. You'll be busy enough teaching that political science course at Greenfield College, and presiding over the Teaparty, and keeping your oar in at the Bayard Foundation, to say nothing of your lectures and being on the board of governors at Adaams Park—

"You have such a curious look on your face. What is it?" Channing looked up over his half-moon glasses, his hazel eyes twinkling as he ruffled through their passports and tickets as the car inched through the snowy lines toward their airline's door.

"Did I? Sorry. I was thinking about closets."

# Perce

Perceval Guy Evelyn Adaams Giffard sat reading Isaiah in Greek by candlelight in the vast, galleried library at Adaams Park. He liked the library; dinnertime he had it all to himself and gave his fantasy that it was his alone full rein. It was one of his privileges to be served in front of the library fire rather than eat with the staff in their small, pleasant dining room downstairs. Especially now that his successor, young whatshisname, had arrived. Nice enough chap, but six hours a day with the boy was enough reminder that he was now, officially, an old man of sixty-five, soon to be put out to pasture. Let the lad form his friendships with the staff at dinner without having to worry about stepping on my toes, Perce thought, pouring out a glass of port.

He'll soon find how little leeway there is here for some of his experimental plans. Perce remembered all too well how he himself had chafed forty-three years ago, when he was a quietly eager twenty-two, at the do's and don'ts of the trusts, endowments, and boards of governors that old Schuyler Adaams had set into being. Nothing could be changed, altered, reupholstered, rebound, restored, or rehung without six different yeses or nos being obtained. Just as well, Perce saw now with the perspective of decades, but the new lad would have to learn for himself it was all for the best. If it hadn't been for Schuyler's seemingly paranoid provisions, Adaams Park would have been destroyed long ago either by real estate developers or by the inroads of the family itself. Each generation was larger, and earning less, wanting more and more of

less and less capital. Most of them, long ago, would have sold
off the Park in order to send their children to Harvard without having to forgo their winters in Jamaica.

As it was, the house—a great stone mansion with a widow's
walk on the banks of the Housatonic, its rolling acres still
manicured to a fare-thee-well—had been left not to the family
at all, but to the world, or as near enough as made no matter,
Perce liked to think. His own contribution, coming in on the
heels of old Huberman in 1926, had enhanced it beyond all
compensation. Perce liked to think, and knew that it was
with much justification, that he had made Adaams Park the
Ditchley of the United States.

Born as the product of one of the Adaams daughters who
had been overlooked and unchaperoned long enough to have
married an unpropertied Englishman, she had produced Perceval in 1904, and rid herself of the Englishman and his
debts, which took most of her own fortune, shortly after. Perceval had a poor sword arm for the modern world and after
Charterhouse, his mother preferring England for them until
the shame back home wore off a bit, and Harvard, had tucked
himself quite happily out of sight at Adaams Park with the
title of Curator and Librarian, which provided him with a
small salary, a guest cottage on the grounds, and the services
of a retired Major of the Marine Corps who ran the mechani-
cal end of things. Perce went slowly, at first, until he saw
what the gaps were and how best they could be filled. He
then began upon the ample acquisition funds left by
Schuyler; during the twenties and thirties he had added to the
library with shrewdness, finesse, and balance. Now any biog-
rapher, genealogist, or historian of New England from the
Civil War, when the first Adaams brothers had taken over
their father's paper mill and started Adaams and Adaams,
publishers of religious, educational, medical textbooks, then
high-minded fiction when the market and the writers appeared, found even a meager week at Adaams Park to be es-

sential to their work. The accommodations were untouched from Schuyler's time, with the exception of separate cloak-rooms for visiting days downstairs and an elaborate fire-alarm system and modern lighting for the paintings.

Schuyler had stipulated convenings, if not conventions, as well as scholarship. Conferences now competed for time at Adaams Park, seminars, executive level meetings of eminent associations. Perce had power, and quickly developed a keen eye for a rip-off, a phony, someone whose proposed biogra-phy of an obscure industrialist was very likely a fruitless front for an inexpensive month in the country. He also developed strong epistolary contacts with historical and genealogical societies all over the world; it gave him pleasure to put up vis-iting members in the great mahogany bedrooms of the main house, to have dinner served in the vast dining room, coffee and port here in the library, its three galleries soaring up to a tooled-leather ceiling barely visible in the flickering light from a fireplace large enough to hold an entire bathroom.

His own little house behind the azalea garden had been full of books too, ones he had acquired from his salary as best he could over the years. Now they were packed, waiting to go to Beemeadows with him. He remembered, suddenly closing the finely bound testaments over his finger for a moment, how Terry had been overawed by his little library when she had seen it for the first time—and it had been only a third the size it was now. Or pretended she had been overawed. Terry. He had been coming across the lawn after a strenuous session with the board of governors, a pallid, vitiated forty-four in a rumpled seersucker suit and white buck shoes, his hair already thinning and going and never more than hair-colored at best, his little potbelly already firmly established.

He'd turned from the path to cut across the long lawn, found her sunbathing. Not that she needed to; her skin was unmistakably Iberian, even the soles of her feet. That gar-dener Vasco's daughter, of course, home from the convent, suddenly grown up. Teresa. "Are you an Adaams?" he'd remembered her saying with awe. "A *real* Adaams?" He may have measured out his life in coffee spoons, except for those three years, but once he had dared to eat a peach. His wedding ring, barely scratched, had been buried with her.

A real Adaams. Now, in his seventh decade, he still did not know what that meant. Terry had known, but he couldn't bear to think of that. What was a real Adaams? The family was so vast now, its past generations so full of Supreme Court justices, college presidents, bishops, a president of the stock exchange, even a few who began to ignore Edith Wharton's generation's observation about politics that "a gentleman simply stayed at home, and abstained" and had gone on to the state house, become diplomats.

Perce had mixed feelings when he waxed a bit gleeful that the great days were over, the younger generations running out of distinction and drive; not much that was promising was coming up in the family that he could see. Adaams & Adaams itself had been bought up a dozen years ago, and just in the nick of time from the looks of their annual report, by one of the enormous conglomerates, was publishing fat novels that were made into long movies. It no longer automatically provided jobs for young Adaamses just out of school. Not that they wanted them, either—scattered all over, out west, California, Chicago, their grandparents' town houses converted to apartments or torn down long ago. Perce still anguished over one twice-removed cousin who had seen a good thing coming and become the real estate czar of Fire Island, most successfully in Cherry Grove. Yes, if there were room for *that* in the family, there was room for a scholar as well.

Channing had showed promise, right from the beginning in marrying Louisa, for one thing. Brains and breeding, Louisa. Channing had all of his mother's drive and looks, too, muscles, vibrancy, virility, the coloring of a lion. And all Marguerite's ambition. Perce sighed, remembering the old lady's

long decline upstairs here at the Park. Even in her most se-
nile, vegetative years she had been a far stronger force than
Perce, and made life hell for everybody. Nobody should take
that long to die, years of nurses round the clock and doctors
brought in from Boston—wicked.

He finished his port slowly, watching the last log burn
down behind the spark guard. Would he miss all this? Not
much choice. Not any choice. Where does a retired scholar—
a good one, but unpublished save for an odd monograph or
two in obscure journals—go? A furnished room near a library
in Hartford? His small pension, his Social Security, and an
odd spot of genealogical research from generous colleagues his
only fortune now. No. He goes to his family. To Beemeadows
Farm.

Would Channing have gotten so involved in these last
years by the idea of a community, community living, if he
and Louisa had had children? Or was this just one of the
many phases in his life, and once he'd mastered it, would he
move on to something else? If it worked at all, for however
long a time, Perce shrewdly guessed it would be more because
of Louisa than Channing—she was a sticker, through and
through.

He opened the Bible to John and philosophically continued reading. "When thou wast young, thou girdest thyself,
and walkdst whither thou wouldst: but when thou shalt be
old, thou shalt stretch forth thy hands, and another shall gird
thee, and carry thee whither thou wouldst not."

# The Russells

Thelma Russell woke to her dream of heart's desire. Late October on East Seventy-second Street, nine-thirty of a Monday morning, and Ray still asleep in the big bed beside her. The top of his head was still a bit sunburned, and the creased back of his neck that always smelled so good. The telephone extension was deliciously, deliriously unplugged, there were theater, opera, ballet tickets on the desk in the library.

Best of all, no grumpy old Flora moaning about her arches and arthritis in the kitchen. They had let her go, after thirty years with them in the little maid's room behind the kitchen in the big old co-op, when they had left for their round-the-world cruise to celebrate Ray's early retirement from the investment counseling firm he had done so well in since they came together from Ohio long ago. Around the world they had gone, their two children happily living their own lives, one married and in North Carolina, the other showing signs of becoming a student emeritus, on yet one more graduate program, this time in Peru.

Seeing the world from a scandalously self-indulgent suite on the ship, the months had idled by in continual summer. No suitcases every night, which they both loathed; the ship provided couriers and porters for all that when it stopped at the interesting places for the curious and adventurous to go inland for a few days. Marvelous. And no telephone! A quiet steward might slip an invitation from a fellow passenger to a cocktail party, lunch, bridge under the door of their suite from time to time, but no telephone there either.

And the food, the amazing variety of diets catered to and presented with such elegance. Even that nice old man from Rotterdam who could eat only grated carrots and yogurt—they were served arranged in a different design, grated differently, a different dish holding shaved ice, the entire time. Well, of course a cruise like that, that cost the earth, would have mostly gall bladder, salt-free, hardening-of-the-arteries, you-name-it diets, but still the crew had avoided any aura of the ship being the S.S. *Geriatrica*. There had been movies, games, classes in everything from hula to history.

Thelma Russell had been bored to tears.

And what's worse, she thought, closing the bathroom door quietly behind her and looking into the mirror, I'm bored to tears now. To say nothing of Ray. If I have to get into my girdle and go sit in another restaurant eating food I don't want and could have better at home, and see another play that's so like the ones we saw twenty years ago we can't tell them apart, I think I will simply expire. All ballet does is make me sad—it's so beautiful, the dancers are so young, and all I can think of is how dreadful it'll be for *them* when they're my age. Dear heaven, if it's hard for me to look at the varicose veins and stretch marks and wattling chin, it must be sheer hell for a dancer to have to give up when they're just beginning to learn what it's all about.

Ray. Thelma knew that for herself she could, by picking up a telephone, instantly reimmerse herself into the life she'd left: charity thrift-shop management for the hospital, fundraising fairs for the kids' old schools, stuffing and licking envelopes for more good causes than she could remember. But for retired men, daytime New York was the ultimate insult. The cronies of yore had no time for lunch with Ray now; lunch was work in Wall Street. And even when they came to dinner there was a subtle but distinct lessening of attention when Ray spoke of anything at all—he was no longer in with the movers and shakers, a nice guy, sure, but out of it now.

How many galleries full of black on white canvases, how many long lunches with him in Chinatown, luxurious first-run movies in the uncrowded afternoons, cherry blossoms on a weekday at the Botanical Gardens, late waffles at home, rainy afternoons in second-hand bookstores with her would make up a life for him? Or her?

She coiled her rusty thick hair into a bun, liking the gray strands that were beginning to tone down the once flaming red. Tiptoing through the bedroom, she smiled at the carpet they had bought in Kairouan; it had an interior sunlight of its own despite the drawn shades and curtains. Through the long parquet hallway, big enough for a bowling alley—she remembered the kids playing shuffleboard long ago on rainy days—to the kitchen. Really, it's ridiculous, this apartment, wonderful when the children were here and we had Dad and his nurse with us for so long too, and Flora, of course, and Miss Kay to come in to do the heavy work, but now? Five bedrooms, a library, two maids' rooms, dining room, drawing room, laundry, four baths?

Poor old Flora, Thelma thought, wishing her all happiness in Sunshine City. Ray had pensioned her handsomely, and the old woman had gladly left them and the huge old-fashioned kitchen that Thelma had never really had to cope with. No wonder Flora'd grumbled so—it was simply impossible, everything was miles apart. Rip it all out, get a kitchen designer in—but for what? Well, it would keep Ray busy for a few months.

Pushing that thought down as both panicky and unworthy, she took her coffee into the living room, picking up the mail in the hall as she went. Circulars, pleas, a mailing from an old P.T.A.—would they never stop? She threw them all in the wastebasket. I will not. It had been fine, that life, but I am fifty-five years old, my children are grown, I have given of myself until I am utterly empty just at the time Ray needs someone most. And right now I wouldn't be a bit surprised if he

went out and found a little bit of fluff—he's just at the age for it anyway, the flattery and excitement and diversion of some-one to make him feel still young and powerful himself. She'd seen him looking overlong at that beautiful, really beautiful, thirty-year-old at dinner last night. She'd held the hands of so many of her women friends as they lived through it, ending up more often than not with estrogen and alimony. Even though Ray'd hate it, she laughed to herself. The surrep-titious hotels and the leers of afternoon desk clerks, or the lady's doorman, and finding restaurants for lunch where he wouldn't be likely to run into friends of her own, and in-genuously giving Thelma a Friday afternoon subscription to the Philharmonic—if the lady were married—to keep her out of his hair. He was too open and honest and Midwestern still to enjoy that part of it, and besides, he'd be lousy at it too. But I wouldn't blame him, though. Of course I'd *murder* him, but I wouldn't blame him.

Oh, how nice—a letter from the Adaamses.

Thelma dear,

The fall colors this morning made me think of your hair, and then how long since we've seen you. If you can bear the thought of even so short a trip after just going around the world, Beemeadows is just now a marvel of warm days, cold nights, and color. Won't you and Ray come for a stay? For the first time in all the years you've been here I can promise you'll be really warm. The fur-nace is at long last brought up to date—with the last pair of Marguerite's earrings, praise be—and even I cannot be-lieve what a difference it makes. (Do you remember the morning you woke up and found your toothpaste had frozen overnight?) So many changes, all good. We've been here three years now, Perce as well, the Scotts and Colonel Bemis in their own houses, and while Channing and I are *still* downstairs in our old rooms we're a-building this spring way up in the far meadow beyond the orchard by the stream and old millpond. Your old rooms upstairs are now enhanced with a little kitchenette for breakfast, a meal which none of us thinks was ever meant to be sociable.

Channing joins me in insisting you come up and see if, after all our talk over the years, you don't think it's a possibility for you. Try to include at least one weekend: Channing is all over the place with various projects, as I knew he would be. Early retirement indeed! He's never been busier, and has taken up pottery on top of everything else. He says it relaxes him, and actually he's quite good. Do come.

Affectionately,

Louisa.

"That from Louisa?" Ray nuzzled the back of Thelma's neck and put his coffee down on the table beside hers. "Good lord, it's ten o'clock. Anything on for today?"

"That new play tonight, the one where everyone's nude, ushers and orchestra and all. Dinner before at the Indonesian restaurant you wanted to try."

"Indonesian? Me? I *hate* Indonesian food." He picked up Louisa's letter and took it to the window. One thing he *could* do today is go over to Sulka's and get a new bathrobe, she thought. My god, how low have we fallen that we fill our days with such desperation.

"Thelma." Ray turned, the sun slanting over his shoulder, holding Louisa's letter.

"Hmm?"

"Let's go. Let's go for good."

## Ada Zipper

Ada Zipper. The dean opened the file before him and quickly ran through the records, going backward to her entrance application last fall. Forty-five, unmarried, twenty-two years secretarial work, the last sixteen with an insurance adjuster in New York. Bronx High. Good grades, high IQ, no application for scholarship help here at Greenfield. Keeping up her class work so far: French I, American Lit, Modern European History, Music Appreciation, Political Science. All freshman classes, except for Adaams', which she was auditing since it was open only to seniors.

He lit his pipe and swiveled back. "Well, Miss Zipper—"

"Ada," she cut in bluntly.

"You're leaving, then? Honestly, my job here is to counsel students, help them make decisions like this, but with you—"

"Yeah, it must be like talking to your aunt." She grinned at him with a face so like an old boot that it was difficult to remember that her figure was very good indeed. He felt every one of his thirty-three years had somehow contained only six months instead of twelve.

"Look, Dean, I'll tell you what. It isn't the college—Greenfield is just fine, but it's me. It's just too late."

"Come on now, Ada. Your grades—"

"Are fine. I know. But grades aren't the point. What I wanted when I came here was—well, I wanted a lot of things, and I still do, but I've found out that some of 'em, like polishing off any more of the rough edges, aren't very realistic, and others don't matter much any more. I got this far in life without knowing why Hester wore an A, and now that I know, it doesn't seem to be very important. Professor Adaams' class is the most real to me—*that* guy knows the nuts and bolts of life, the way it's all a game, really—same thing in the insurance racket. Look, Dean, suddenly last year I realized probably half my life's over, more'n half, really, and I start to think about what the hell am I doing, pounding a typewriter and screaming into a phone all day, year after year, for a boss whose ulcers make his guts look like the craters on the moon. And then it really grabbed me when one of the dames in the office was retired at sixty-five. Well, she gets a nice little black and white TV from the boss, and a bye-bye bottle party at four-thirty on Friday, and home she goes. A month later she'd stuck her head in the oven because she'd been so scared years ago about retiring she'd changed her age on her pension form and was really seventy-two, and so the crummy pension fund wouldn't pay on a technicality. That really knocked the socks off me. You wanta hear more?"

"You bet."

"Okay, so there I was, all my sisters and brothers married, me living with Ma like a good Greek daughter until she died. Jekyll during the day and Hyde at night. Just me, then, old Aunty Ada. A ball-breaking secretary for a ball-breaking boss in a tough racket, and with a style I knew couldn't get me anywhere else, like an uptown job in an ad agency or anything, where they want class. Then it happened."

"What?"

"I couldn't believe it myself." Ada leaned back, closed her eyes. "I won the lottery. . . . Yeah, the state lottery. Well, somebody has to, don't they? When I think I *almost* stopped buying tickets every week when OTB came in—I'm a big horse player, too—well, anyway, it was me, old Ada Zipper of the Ninth Avenue Zippers, née Zipipopolous, with fifty thousand smackers. After taxes."

"Whew! What was the first thing you did?" The dean was oblivious to everything else, the cries of the frisbee players outside his window, his smoldering pipe, the clock on the wall.

"Had a nose job. Boy, you should have seen the big Greek honker I *used* to have! Well, it didn't help much because a beauty I ain't and never will be, but it sure helped in my head. And then I thought, *Ada, this is your time.* You been strap-hanging all your life, one way or another, to and from school, to and from work, to and from the family. The most I'd ever hoped for was to save up enough so I could take Ma back to see the old folks in Athens, but what's the fun in that with Ma dead? I don't know any of them and they're all dying off too. But I thought if I was going to travel, maybe I'd better learn where I was going first. And then the other thing—" Her attention broke, she got up and looked out at the feathery green of the first spring trees.

"The other thing was the country. I'd never been more'n a day or two at a time all my life in the country. So—Greenfield College."

"And?" He watched her sturdy attractive figure turn from the window, plunk down in the chair across his desk. She had beautiful skin.

"Listen, Dean, don't feel bad. One of the best things I've found is what I don't want. That gives me a lot of freedom, you know? Like I said, it's too late to catch up on enough of the culture kick to make much difference, so what the hell. I do know I don't want to go back to New York. Sure, I could get another job, probably the same one back, but there's a million Ada Zippers, there, strap-hanging. Being old Aunty Ada—the one that didn't catch a husband and never will, and had to stay home and take care of the old folks, and gets to put the nieces and nephews on and off the bus from camp, and wash the dishes at Thanksgiving and Christmas and

Easter, and start watching all the family with an eagle eye to see if there's any signs yet of their waiting for me to die and leave them what's left of my money. Besides, fifty thousand sounds like a lot, but it's funny how dough can be too much and too little isn't it?"

The dean was beginning to feel he was having a very indelible experience. "Found anything you do like that's surprised you?"

"Yeah. Two things. Driving! Never drove a car in my life till I got up here, and you know what, I'm darn good! Love it. And the other thing—oh, boy, I just love the country. All year long, mud season and all. There ain't no way I'm not gonna live in the country. I went over to Pittsfield to see about a job, but it's already too much of a town—even Lee's too big. I know, I know"—she held up a square, thick hand—"what can I do but office work? I don't know. I'm tight enough with my dough so that now I've had my fling, I figure a nice safe five-six per cent will help, but it won't do the whole thing. I've seen some of the big estate places around, at least the gates and driveways, and I wouldn't mind being a caretaker or a maid even, but frankly, I've never been around nice furniture and rugs and china and all that. I mean, I don't know if I could do it. And I can't cook worth beans, Ma did all that." She chewed on a fingernail.

"Don't sell yourself short, Ada. I have a distinct feeling you could do anything you put your mind to. But do one thing first, will you? For yourself?"

"Ah, Dean, don't try and talk me into finishing the year out—I know the tuition ain't refundable and that's a pang, I can tell you, but I'm finished here. Now."

"I know. No, what I had in mind was someone who might be able to give you a better steer than I can, a man who knows the area a lot better than I do—you've been auditing his course anyway—Adaams, Channing Adaams. He's started a semiretirement community over in Chetford, he and his wife, three or four years ago. With people like you—at least in some ways. Ready for a new phase in their lives. I think you should talk to him, go over and give it a look and let it give a look at you. It may be just what you want, for a while, anyway."

## Sally and Webster Hayward

Hayward & Hayward
Organizational Development
379 East 31st St.
New York, N.Y. 10016

Sally to Webster:

"—and of course Channing's continuing consultative status at the Bayard Foundation has been of great benefit to us. From your last letter I think you're handling their problem quite well. It fits in perfectly with our plan for your replacing Channing there when the time comes—he's been there far too long and doing nothing. I'll join you for their executive-level conference in May, of course."

Sally Webster lit a mentholated cigarette and turned on the desk light; Adaams Park was always gloomy and the spring rain made it more so. "I'm returning the agenda for the South Americans; by and large I think it is well structured, but as you see, I've changed the timing during the middle of the day on Wednesday. You really *must* give them more than forty-five minutes for lunch, at least an hour. They don't expect a siesta, but too short a time and they come to the afternoon session with great hostility which is an efficient use of time overcoming.

"Adaams Park much improved in facilities now that old fossil Perceval is gone—ample easels, projectors, recorders, and so on. He was so stubborn about that. I've even been given a room in the main house itself, which is a great convenience. Never forget my first visits here when I was beginning with Dreiser—a room over the garage. Glad this three days with the Am. Assn. Adv. Science soon over—Park getting very booked up; senior officials of the UN scheduled next week to rewrite Breton Woods Agreements. Channing will undoubtedly be in on that one way or another.

"About Webby's tuition and therapist's bill: we *did* budget for them in January; it was the initial down payment to the orthodontist and the Ronkonkoma Aircraft job falling through, plus the bill for water damage to those people underneath our apartment, that's thrown things out of kilter. Particularly important after the bathtub mishap and the other things that Webby not feel we're rejecting him by sending him to camp this summer. Dr. Blanford feels very strongly on this, particularly since I am away so much. We must *find* the money for camp; it will be far cheaper, for instance, to accept Channing's invitation to a trial summer at Beemeadows and send Webby to Vermont than for the three of us to rent at the beach again, for instance. Unfortunately that Colonel Bemis has to be in Albany with his father—dying—the father —and Channing has found a student from Greenfield to rent Bemis' cabin, so we'll have to be in the main house but can have the entire top floor to ourselves, perfect conditions for finishing the book. (The title still is tricky: 'New Models for Organizational Development: Theory & Practice'?)

"Of course I know Channing expects us to make a real contribution of our organization management skills; it'll be interesting to see how that community is shaping. It may do very well for us in a few years when Webby goes to boarding school. After all, we both saw fifty last year—it *was* wise to put off having Webby until that woman remarried and you were free of alimony, although I know you didn't think so at the time. But he's nine now, and it won't be too long until we'll want to make some plans for our future; all the more reason to look into Beemeadows this summer. Will you send in his camp application? I thought I brought it with me but remember now it's in the office in Webby's files.

"I know how you balked investing in video tape but it's *most* successful—I'm starting them off with the jigsaw puzzles with missing pieces tomorrow and the instant replay will show them their aggressions and hostilities better than a thousand words. It's already earning enough to pay us back four times over.

"Webby will leave for camp the 15th of June so we'll have a good ten weeks at the farm. Will be in Chicago Friday; write to me there."

\*

Dear Sally,

The agenda for the South Americans got here, you were right about the lunch hour, as always. Did you ever write to the insurance company about their not paying the $1,400 damages? Still can't see how an overflowing bathtub could have done that much to wallpaper or whatever it was.

Agree about Beemeadows on all levels, especially as a chance to feel around Channing and the Bayard job. Also, it'll be interesting to see what patterns have been established in the last five years there and need correcting. The weekends we've had have been pleasant, but we both know how deceptive party manners are. You'll be in a great position to clear that all up—unless you'd rather put full time on the book and have me take on the community.

Webby has just come in from school and wants to add a line; hope this gets to Chicago before you do. See you next week.

Webster

dEar SAlly ) bRing Me a presnt backFrom Shickawgo

weBBY

## Miss Priscilla Buckham

"Giffard. That's the connection. The Bedes and Giffards are all tangled up over there in England somewhere around the Civil War—ours, not yours—your cousin Perceval sent me this genealogy a few years ago, just before he left Adaams Park and went to Beemeadows." The old woman laid the bound folder on a tilt-top table in her dim drawing room in Old Greenwich and, taking her nephew's arm, balanced her weight between her strength and a new, shining lucite cane, descending the low stone steps beyond the open french door to a breakfast table under a flowered awning.

"Interesting—I do recall a porringer sent by one of the old great-aunts, it had the Giffard crest on it. Used to bang it about frightfully, I'm afraid, and so did my son when he was a tad." Simon Bede pulled out his aunt's chair with a square, strong hand, helped the ancient housemaid, whose starched uniform and apron seemed to be holding her upright as much as her frail musculature, get his aunt settled comfortably.

"Yes, well. As long as you're here and touring the East it's time you saw some of your American relations other than me. I called Perceval this morning before you were up and told him you and your friend would be in Great Bedford tonight at the Black Griffon; he invited you to tea this afternoon on your way. Beemeadows isn't far from there; he said to stop in the general store in Chetford for directions. And of course Perceval's cousin—if we were Southerners and went in for all those distant connections, which we don't, he'd be a distant cousin of yours as well—where was I? Oh, yes. Channing

Adaams is a very interesting man; I went to school with his wife's mother, Laura Anstruther. Poor thing, died when her daughter was born."

"Very good of you to think of it, Aunt Priscilla; of course we'll stop for tea. Don't fret—" The old lady was peering out from under the umbrella, looking from side to side. "Helen's around having a love affair in the rose garden. She has a new lens and there's a half-opened peace rose. She'll be along. She can smell a corn muffin at fifty paces. . . ."

"Very well—serve Father Bede now, Mildred, and then bring us some of that jam you made."

The old maid crackled off toward the nether regions, leaving the coffeepot on the table and their plates filled. "Now, Simon," and he recognized a cautionary note in his aunt's voice, "are you sure you're not doing yourself and the Church a great disservice, touring about the country with this Miss Bullock? I know times have changed, but *that* much?—and for a man of the cloth? What will your bishop think?"

"My bishop, Aunty, is so absorbed—and rightly so—in his own divorce I doubt he'd have much interest in my holiday plans right now. And you remember, dear, I'm retired, Lambeth knows me not nor e'er will again. My stint is o'er."

"Humph. Bit young for that, aren't you? Fifty and a bit? Well, I suppose you know best. Maybe this Miss Bullock'll be good for you after all—she's certainly made something of herself. Tried to get her new book on the Galápagos Islands from the library when I heard you were coming. Librarian said there was a waiting list a dozen names long. Not that you haven't come far, my dear, aide to the archbishop and all that. Such a pity to stop there. But then—"

She stopped. A woman was coming around the corner of the house wearing a T-shirt and denim skirt and sneakers, a much-worn canvas bag slung over her shoulder, camera strap hanging out of the top and one leg of a tripod poking through a hole in the canvas.

"You're very fond of her, aren't you, Simon?"

"She's a very fondable lady, Aunty P." Simon, his blue eyes warming, pulled out a chair for Helen and laid the camera bag carefully on a bench.

"That Mildred—Simon, move Miss Bullock's place, she's in the sun—"

"Please, Miss Buckham, I love it. Sorry to be late, but the rose was irresistible. It owed me something, anyway. The scent of them coming in my window almost kept me awake last night. Awfully nice of you to let us stay, much more fun to start our rambles clean and rested instead of doing the usual getting-out-of-New-York-battle first thing."

"My pleasure. Mildred, give Father Bede that jam and serve Miss Bullock." She peered at Simon's friend, curious at the difference between her and Simon's wife, killed years ago in a dreadful automobile smash. Anthea had been typically English, fair, petal-skinned. This Bullock woman—well, perhaps the modern "complexion" was the lack of one, but she was actually weather-beaten, swarthy almost. And her hair: every known color of brown with a driftwood frosting running through it, and the wisps around her ears and the back of her neck looked as if a goat had been nibbling at it. Good figure, though, nice legs and ankles and wrists. Lovely smile, too, twinkly brown eyes and one front tooth that was slightly crooked but somehow added to her charm rather than took away from it.

Simon looked happy, happier and better than in years, losing his hair a bit but all the Bedes did and it didn't detract a bit from their warm, quiet attractiveness. He wasn't so harassed as the last time she'd seen him, he stood taller; it seemed to her as if the flow of what he gave out was finally being balanced by his letting a reciprocal flow come in. Not depleted.

"—think you can stand an extremely distant cousin or two?" he was asking Helen. "We were going to try for Great Bed-

ford tonight anyway, and Aunt Priscilla tells me I've familial
skeletons near there on a farm in a place called Chetford. She
called them and booked us for tea this afternoon."

"Skeletons indeed, Simon." Priscilla almost rapped her new
cane on the flagstones. "Can't imagine anyone calling Perceval
Giffard a skeleton in the closet, much less Channing
Adaams."

"Adaams?" Helen put down her coffee cup, took half a
muffin off Simon's plate. "I met him once donkey's years ago
down in Central America—*Globe* sent me down for a revo-
lution in the late fifties. He was there with the UN, doing a
terrific job."

"That's the one. Aunt Priscilla tells me he's running a variety of early retirement community up in the Berkshires; the
closer cousinship is with Perceval Giffard, I can't really claim
Channing Adaams although I've heard of him often, of
course. Tea near Chetford fit in, Madam Tour Director?"

"Sure, why not. Channing Adaams out to pasture? He was
cutting quite a swath at the Bayard Foundation a few years
ago. Can't imagine him mulching turnips or whatever. Is
Cousin Giffard the one who used to run Adaams Park? Pass
the jam, Simon. I did a take-out on that for the old mag once;
it reminded me of Ditchley."

"Now that's a nice compliment, Miss Bullock, you be sure
to tell him so. I sensed from one of his letters several years
ago when he moved to Beemeadows that it was quite a
wrench to leave the Park. However, we all come to the end of
things one way or another. By the way, dearie, I must say I
like my new cane. Very kind of you both. Simon, d'you think
it's too frivolous for church?"

"Not a bit of it!" He took it from her, held it in front of
him, letting the sun play through the clear plastic. "Cantuar
had a lucite primatial staff, don't forget, and a gorgeous thing
it was. Helen found the cane at that place on Fifty-seventh
Street."

"Glad you like it, Miss Buckham. Simon, I think I'd better give the Black Griffon a bang on the pipes and tell them to hold our rooms till later; they pull them out from under you if you don't show up by four. Excuse me."

"Now, Simon, I want to hear more about your boy Fergus—"

*

Waving the cane in farewell as their little car scooted away, around the circle of azaleas in the drive, Miss Buckham stood for a moment looking at the inexorable sundial in the midst of the green shrubs. Better—yes, it *was* better—that her nephew had that bright, comfortable, accepting woman with him than for him to be alone. *And* he seemed to have the sense to know his own good fortune. Much better for him than to end up as she herself was, with only azaleas to be grateful for.

# CHAPTER I

Helen fought off waking up, knowing she wasn't going to like it for some reason or other. Much better to fit into the feathers again. If she lay very still the warmth Simon had left behind in his side of the big old bed would last a bit longer. A window shade sucked and flapped slightly, disturbing the shadow-boxing of a horsefly.

She dreamed someone was beating, systematically and thoroughly, a child outside the window. Waking, she realized someone *was* beating a child outside the window, quite thoroughly, and the little monster's roars and yells of rage were not deterring the beater. "There, just remember *that* for the rest of your stay here, young man. Someone should have done that for you years ago. No wonder that camp in Vermont sent you back—at least you know now you can't behave like a menace to the human race here."

Helen ground her head back into the pillows, remembering bits of yesterday. Channing Adaams' voice continued. "Now take this shovel and get out there and fill in any other holes you've dug and remove any traps you've set. Don't come back until they're all finished!"

"Sally—SALLLLY! He's hit me, he hit me—"

The electric typewriter in the room above Helen's stopped its throbbing and clicking; a woman's voice called down from the upstairs window:

"Webby, I'm sure you don't mean to interrupt but I'm right in the middle of a very important chapter. We'll discuss it at lunch." The window closed.

Oh, God. Helen opened her eyes, tried to push herself up a bit, and lay back in a sweat as the sprained tendon in her thigh flashed exquisite pain up to her hip. Why was that leg so clammy? She poked at it with her other foot, found the plaster cast rising from foot to knee still damp, cool. That's right, she told herself, wake up and you *won't* like it at all.

She and Simon had left Aunt Priscilla's, getting off the Massachusetts Turnpike at Westfield and wandering along mountain and foothill roads, rivers, rushing streams, referring casually to the road map from time to time, eating Mildred's picnic lunch of tomato sandwiches, deviled eggs, and pound cake by the side of a sunlit stream, wading in sunlit water. It had seemed just as easy to reach Great Bedford and the inn by way of Chetford as any other way, once Helen had found the flyspeck that was Chetford on the map; they had stopped, a bit past four, at the wide spot in the road that had a little firehouse, a small church, a garage, a general store, and a post office.

A lively, plain woman with snapping black eyes had put down a much-marked copy of *The Racing Form* on the store's counter, sized them up, and after giving them directions to Beemeadows asked them if they would take up a bag of groceries. Someone named Thelma had called and said Perce was having a fit and needed them for dinner.

Helen swung the car off the paved road onto a graveled county road with an almost invisible sign that said "To Middlefield"; they entered a green tunnel of tree branches, crossed a rushing brown stream, passed a small log cabin with a giant maple tree shadowing the front porch, a little VW parked behind, and a few hundred yards farther on found the stone pillars marking the entrance to Beemeadows Farm. The main house was a comfortable, ugly sprawl of porches, dormers, els, verandas that could only with laxity be called Dutch Colonial; its skirts of uncut green hay meadows spread out around it on each side and in back, the forested hills rising directly behind a large barn and small outbuildings.

Helen had recognized Channing Adaams instantly among the group sitting in the dappled light on the front veranda. Hadn't changed much at all, she thought, crackling with vitality, stocky, broad-boned, still with that lion's mane of hair. He was wearing a pair of old tennis shorts, came striding with sinewy legs on high-arched bare feet across the grass to welcome them.

Shrewd, too. Sized up Simon instantly as a personage—most people didn't, Helen knew, with that unobtrusive, quiet air of his that so belied his inner strength and bull-dog will. He had led them up to the veranda, regretting he and Simon had narrowly missed each other in Nairobi in '69—or was it '70—Channing there in a double capacity for the Bayard Foundation and as representative for the World Council of Churches, Simon sent out by Lambeth for the Anglican Communion.

A slender, fine-boned dark woman with a white plume in her heavy black hair brushed a long-haired tortoise-shell cat off her lap gently, rose, shook hands. Louisa Adaams. More elegant in a faded denim wraparound and scuffed thong sandals than most women would be after a day at Elizabeth Arden's. A distressingly fat, freckled little boy of about nine darted out from his hiding place under the veranda and ran after the cat across the lawn, waddling from behind. "Webby, be gentle, dear," Louisa called after him. The boy's mother, a short, hefty woman with greasy dark bangs and an ill-advised muumuu, paid no attention but held out her empty glass to her husband while interrupting Simon and Channing.

Perceval Guy Evelyn Adaams Giffard appeared shyly around the corner of the veranda, sporting a threadbare but well-cut blazer far too hot for the afternoon, a pair of flannel bags, an ancient school tie—it was so old, so sad, so ugly, it *has* to be a school tie, Helen thought—and, looking more like a short flannel egg than anything else, let himself be inserted between Channing and Simon and introduced to his English cousin. The three stages of fire, Helen suddenly thought: Channing the gold-red flame, Simon the subtle, lasting hot embers, and Perceval—ash.

Helen wished the man named Hayward, Webster Hayward, who was pouring drinks for everyone, would stop babbling to her about her work, how great the old *Globe* had been, how great her new book was. He'd be asking for her autograph next. Or at least that he'd stop sweating so much.

On the pretext of getting the groceries from the car, Helen wandered off the veranda to the car park behind the barn. The cow stalls had been turned into parking slots for six cars; chickens had their own space and ran in and out querulously. There was a storage stall with an old croquet set, archery butt, rotted badminton net. A workshop scrupulously clean and new, a broken table waiting in an elaborate agony of vises for glue to dry. A garden shed with a small tiller, tools, wheelbarrow.

She wandered on, out of sight of the house. The original chicken house backed against the woods that marched up the steep hillside, one side facing the blazing sun with a small, neat lawn in front. Window boxes, curtains, a double chimney in the middle declared other occupants now; there was a crumbling old brick path leading up to the back of the main house. Jewelweed rampaged from the barn to the chicken house, right up to the shade of the woods in back where fern and moss took over immediately, lining the narrow rutted road leading up into the dark green light. She followed it, breaking through the woods into a new meadow with an old apple orchard at the top, private, secret. Upthrusts of rock broke through the hay, proclaiming New England. She heard a sound of rushing water farther on up in the woods.

Turning back, she followed an old dry-stone wall running down diagonally through the woods, finding a shallow pond of dark brown water hummocked with emerald moss, still and waiting. And along the edge as she neared the house again she had stepped into fat little Webby Hayward's "animal trap," a vicious damp stinking hole the little bastard had dug in the mucky ground, then laid branches criss-cross over the top, covered them with leaves, moss, and ferns. Helen had fallen into it up to her hips, with a sickening twist to her thigh and a strong snap of pain in her foot.

And, before she could get her breath and fight down the nausea that came with pain, she'd seen the little creep hiding in a clump of bracken, his pudgy hand over his mouth but his whole freckled face in a rictus of glee. Until Simon and Channing had come in answer to her yells and gently lifted her out, covered with mud and unable to put any weight on her right leg.

It had been nearly ten by the time the hospital in Pittsfield had X-rayed, bandaged, plastered her, and let her go, provided with pain killers, muscle relaxants, and instructions to lie still for a few days, use crutches and not walk on the cast for the first forty-eight hours. The sprained tendon would be the more painful; the broken bone in her foot would take about four weeks in plaster but after a day or so she wouldn't feel it much.

Channing, who had driven them to the hospital, had insisted they come back to Beemeadows; Helen could never manage the narrow stairs at the Black Griffon to begin with, there were extra empty rooms on the ground floor of the main house—the Adaamses' old rooms, actually—Helen could get about easily on one floor. She remembered gratefully letting Simon help her into the high old horsehair-mattressed bed and abdicating all responsibility for herself or anything else as the sleeping pill he made her take very surely knocked her out.

Ten-thirty; Simon had taken off her watch and left it on a file cabinet that served as a bedside table. Helen pulled herself up again, blessing the firm bed as she wincingly swung her legs over its side and fumbled for the crutches propped against the wall. At least she could bend her knee; the cast stopped just below it.

Puffing her way back to bed from the bathroom next door, the tip of one crutch slipped off a gathering of glass marbles and jackstraws and old playing cards halfway under the bed and went skittering out from under her. She fell forward, abandoning the other crutch in order to break the fall with her hands, and knocked over a pile of finely woven old baskets that was precariously perched on top of a stack of cardboard cartons. An assortment of smaller baskets spilled out around her, a primitive flute, a shell- and bead-adorned ritual mask, feathered and boned artifacts, pouches, ankle bracelets tumbled out, mixing with the toys and crutch under the bed.

"Oh, my dear!" Louisa Adaams must have knocked and Helen not heard; she came in sideways through the door from the next room, carrying a breakfast tray. "Helen! Do be careful!" Propped on one arm, Helen saw she was white as a sheet under her sallow skin, almost dropping the tray on the bed before rushing forward and beginning to scoop up the smaller objects indiscriminately, playing cards and masks and bracelets and jackstraws and marbles and stuffing the toys in her pockets, the rest in one of the larger baskets.

"Sorry," Helen panted, trying to clamber up to at least a kneeling position as Louisa's thin long hand swept up the last of the treacherous toys from under Helen's cast. My heaven, she's almost shaking, Helen thought. "I hope I didn't break anything, I'm not in practice with crutches and hooked on a marble—"

"My dear, I didn't mean Channing's baskets and things, I mean you—I'm so terribly sorry. Webby must have been playing in here and left his things—" She set all the baskets in one and put them on top of an old highboy in the corner, rolled up two slippery rag rugs and shoved them under the bed. She helped Helen stand up, get back in bed, put a hard pillow behind her back, and pulled the breakfast tray closer.

"On top of everything else, you poor thing—" Louisa's breathing was quieter, she deftly pulled up the soft old quilt, raised the window shades enough so that the top half of the room was still dim and soothing, the old oak floor glowing with sun. "I do hope Channing's confrontation with Webby outside didn't wake you—the poor child's been so lonesome here, I'm afraid. We aren't really organized for children, but Webby threw a brick at his counselor the first week in camp and was sent back. I'm sure he's dreadfully sorry about your leg; I'll have to speak to him again about leaving his toys about."

Helen, reveling in the excellent coffee, doubted the boy's grief, remembering his gleeful face watching her struggling in his damn muddy animal trap.

"Marvelous coffee—won't you have some?" Helen finessed.

"Just did, thank you. That's all Channing's pottery on your tray, by the way. His latest hobby, he's gotten very good, or at least I think so." Louisa sat in a low wicker chair by the window, her hands in the pockets of the old Liberty print smock whose pattern faded into the still more faded wallpaper of the room. "I've sent your friend Simon up to our house with Channing for a heating pad; it'll help the sprain, they're agony. Such a shame to have to put you here in this—archive —" She looked around ruefully at the orderly cardboard boxes lining the wall, the faded space on the wallpaper where photographs or pictures had hung, the missing chest of drawers. "We're slowly getting this all either thrown away or moved into our new little house up in the woods, but Channing refuses to take one single thing up that hasn't been cleaned or repaired or filed or weeded out properly, and you can imagine thirty-five years of souvenirs and papers and clippings—to say nothing of the results of his photography period! Of course he's right and it's far easier for me to do it here; as long as I work next door anyway, but hard on you. I'll try to find some pretty sheets to cover them up."

"You should see my apartment in New York, Louisa; I never get quite unpacked and there's always luggage all over the place. I feel quite at home."

"You're a dear. I can at least take those South American things Channing's been saving for years up with me this morning; we're going to hang them over the fireplace wall and always meant to." She pulled a man's shirt out of the basket arm of the rocker, began sewing up a tear across the yoke. "It's wonderful to have our own place at last; we'd always planned for these rooms to be used for guests eventually, and for an office, so even the first few years we've been here, until we built this spring, have been *en poste* so to speak. I'm feeling terribly bridal now that we're actually living in it."

You don't look bridal, Helen thought. You look hollowed out, ravaged. Worse than when you came in and found me on the floor, and a disaster area compared to yesterday on the porch.

"Tell me more about Beemeadows—I know Channing and Simon and you were talking about it when I went for my ill-fated stroll; do you each have your own houses, then?"

"More or less—finally. Channing and I were the last to build, I knew we would be. He's so very busy, of course, and I'm afraid I drew the job of—well, quartermaster, administrator, whatever." She cleared her throat softly; her voice was pleasant, low, a bit hoarse, attractive. She tucked the shirt into the arm of the rocker, began sorting through folders of old snapshots as she talked, writing dates, locations, on them. "We each have our own jobs of course. Thelma Russell—you haven't met her yet—discovered she had an incredible talent for kitchen gardening; you'll see at dinner tonight. And Simon's cousin Perce is another revelation, especially to himself. He'd scarcely seen a saucepan all his life, but he's turned into the most incredible cook and simply loves it! Won't let anyone else into the kitchen."

"Do you all eat together, then?"

"Only dinner—Ada, for instance, couldn't be here for luncheon in any event, and we're all so busy with different things during the day it wouldn't work too well. It's quite pleasant; we don't see too much of each other, and of course from time to time some of us aren't here at all—the Scotts, for instance, are away this summer in New Mexico on a dig, they're anthropologists, and Channing of course is all over the place all the time—Boston, New York, lecturing, his seminars at Greenfield College, and so forth. Perce is busier than he wants to be with genealogies for rich Texans just now, and of course Thelma's husband, Ray, is the definitive handyman of the world. Thelma swore he was allergic all his life to anything with handles, never so much as changed a light bulb, but he holds the whole place together in terms of storm windows and compost heaps and window glazing and anything that needs to be fixed. He loves it. And of course he does the really elaborate quarterly bookkeeping and tax forms and so on, I just hold the figures together for him."

"You said something about an Ada?"

Louisa snapped a rubber band around a dozen sorted and dated packets of snapshots, tucked it in place in a fresh carton at her feet. "You would have met her when you stopped at the store in Chetford. Ada Zipper—a bit younger than the rest of us, about your age I'd think, and something of a rough diamond, but absolutely genuine and we all love her. She and Perce live back to back in the old chicken house. She'd been a city woman all her life, and none of us was sure if she'd fit in or how she'd keep busy here, but she's a walking example of Providence. No sooner had she gotten here than the Schmichaels, who had run the general store in Chetford for years, poor Mr. Schmichael came down with dreadful emphysema;

Ada stepped in on a friendly neighbor basis to give Mrs.
Schmichael a hand. Well, he died and his wife went over to
live with her daughter in Cooperstown, and Ada came into
her own. She's buying them out on a time arrangement Ray
Russell and she figured out; she's a very intelligent business-
woman as well as being the salt of the earth. She gets along
wonderfully well with the locals, too, which is a great help
right now."

"Beemeadows having city-slicker cliché problems?"

"Near enough. It's the zoning—Alf Bemis, the Colonel,
was working on that with our little zoning board, but his father's dying of cancer and poor Alf's living in Albany with
him this summer. You'd like him, he's an ex-army engineer
and keeps us all in firewood and plows out the snow in our
driveways in the winter. He's also a splendid cabinetmaker,
he's doing quite well with selling his things through an outlet
in Boston. Ah, there you are!" The large long-haired tortoise-
shell cat of yesterday strolled into the room disdainfully, allowed itself to jump up into Louisa's lap, settled there firmly
convinced it was doing Louisa a signal honor. "This is
Magnificat; she belongs to the college girl Channing found to
rent Alf's cabin for the summer—she's like Ada was, this cat,
a city girl who found out she loves the country. Always bringing in dead mice and moles and things. Katey—Alf's tenant—
works at night at the bar in the Black Griffon and worries
about Magnificat getting lost or hurt, but so far she's had a
wonderful time. Good heavens, I thought I'd sorted all these
and was ready to paste them up—these are *years* ago—"

Louisa fanned out a yellowing envelope full of old snapshots and negatives, her fist clenched over one, the sunlight
pouring in on the suddenly still rocker, her profile frozen in
silhouette. Helen could hear the cat's purr, her own watch
ticking on the file cabinet by the bed, wished she could ask
for more coffee.

"Excuse me—" Louisa didn't seem to know to whom she

was speaking; she put the envelope neatly in the basket arm
of the old rocker, pushed herself with clenched fists slowly up
from the chair, and, running one hand along the wall for support, walked stiffly into the bathroom. Helen heard her
drawing a glass of water. A brown plastic medicine phial
rolled out across the sill, spilling white tablets which Helen
thought were her own Demerol until she saw the hospital's
bottle on the bedside cabinet next to her watch. Louisa's
hand reached down, swept them up from the floor, withdrew.
She must hurt like hell, then; the doctor at the hospital had
given Helen only four Demerol tablets "for extreme pain,"
with a more lavish dispensation of codeine in another bottle
for "ordinary pain."

"Sorry." She came back to the rocker slowly, her face a
dreadful putty color, her voice a soft rasp, unable to disguise a
spasm of pain as she lowered herself into the rocker. "I seem
to have received one of the rewards of reaching fifty-six this
spring. Arthritis. I don't recommend it."

"Can I get you anything?" Helen felt like the blind leading
a Seeing Eye dog, feeling for her crutches with one foot.

"No, please, don't move. Give me a minute; those pills
work quite fast, really." Helen suspected it was more good
breeding than the Demerol she had just taken that was bringing her back to their conversation; wished she wouldn't. "It's
just as well Thelma has a green thumb after all; the garden
was what I always dreamed of when we finally had a place to
call home, and now with my legs and ankles in this state I'd
not be able to do it at all. I did get my white roses planted
this spring—you'll see them, they're all along the front of the
house. So lovely. Where were we? Oh, yes, Katey—such a
pretty girl, we all wish we could see more of her; she does
have the afternoons to herself but seems to like to be alone.
Her parents are in Pakistan for the year; she seems a bit—
lost."

"It must be damn hard work to be young these days."

Helen began to babble deliberately to give Louisa a rest. "Too many choices. When I was a kid her age the limits were so outrageously hypocritical it was perfectly easy to say to hell with them and jump over the walls. But when there aren't *any* walls—ah, here you are, luv."

"Bearing warmth for the wounded." Simon unfolded a king-size heating pad, plugged it in, and helped Helen nudge it in place under her thigh.

"As always." She smiled gratefully at him. "Thanks. Louisa's been making me feel very welcome instead of a terrific bother. I intend to paste up scrapbooks to earn my keep, if Louisa'll let me—I thought you, Father Bede, could be a bit more physical and pluck chickens and bale hay or something."

"Good heavens, Simon"—the color was slowly coming back to Louisa's lips, although her eyes were dull as she stood— "what a distinction that would be, having Helen Bullock paste up Channing's snapshots!"

"She'll love it. It's her metier. Just give her a paste pot and away she goes. Not today, though. I, Dr.—Doctor of Pastoral Theology, Oxon., but Doctor nonetheless—Dr. Bede prescribe a codeine now and a pre-lunch nap."

"Of course." Louisa picked up the breakfast tray. "You're both on vacation, you're meant to enjoy yourselves. There isn't an inn or motel within fifty miles that doesn't have stairs, and we love having you. I'll be back down from our house to see about your luncheon."

"Here, give me that tray." Simon took it from her. "That's one thing I can do. I can also pluck chickens, by the way, and you mustn't disarrange your day to feed us." He sidled out the narrow door through the office to the kitchen.

"Louisa, Simon's a heavenly cook, truly. If Perce'll let him use the kitchen he can go down to the store now and find something for lunch."

"Oh, my dear, Perce never needs the kitchen until three or

four—dinner's at eight—and Thelma picks early in the morning; there'll be a dozen things on the back porch and in the fridge for lunch. Cheese, our own eggs, beer and wine—I'll not come down then until teatime." She reached up slowly, picked up the baskets on top of the highboy.

"Let Simon come up and hang those for you, if you've got dickey ankles—he's awfully good at that sort of thing."

"What a nice thought—Channing does have to go to Pittsfield any minute and I confess ladders are a bit tricky."

"Fine. I'll send him up after lunch."

"So nice of you both—call if you want anything."

*

Simon closed the door behind Louisa, sat down quietly on the bed beside Helen, gently rubbing his thumb along the back of her hand. "Nice Helen."

"Mmmm." A scent of summer puffed in the window. "You going to go bonkers if we stay here for a day or so? I didn't really believe the sawbones last night at the hospital, but I see what he meant about staying flat for a day or so now. It feels —appropriate."

"Of course it does. As for bonkers, not on your nelly. Thelma—you'll like her, a very sophisticated mother earth and handsome as hell—has already recruited me to pick Perce two quarts of blackberries for a tart this afternoon, Ada called to ask if I'd keep store in Chetford tomorrow morning while she goes to the dentist, Channing has invited us both to a personal two-guinea tour of Adaams Park in a few days when he runs over for a meeting—"

"Lawks, what a busy whirl! I volunteered you, by the way, right after lunch to go up and hang up some things for Louisa, she's got arthritis and can't do ladders. What's their little house like, anyway?"

"Not quite so little as I imagine she described it—very

much the self-deprecating Puritan aristocrat, isn't she? Lovely house. Extraordinarily private, all their outposts; the lay of the land is perfect for that, alternating meadows, woods, orchards. Well, let's see." He settled back against the footboard of the bed, the light from the window behind him outlining the fine solid shape of his head and shoulders. "The Adaamses are well up at the top, far beyond where you walked yesterday, the house itself faces south, backs out over an old millstream and pond. Channing's workroom, study, pottery, whatever you call it, is cantilevered out over the pond with a private deck beyond. Lots of double glass, fireplaces, one large bedroom, small kitchen, grasscloth walls—no, the silky kind, *not* plastic—warm-looking in the winter, I'd think. I'll drive you up, very gently I promise, in a day or so."

"Doesn't sound much like Crumbles." Helen yawned. The codeine was taking effect.

They both giggled. Simon's dilapidated little house in England was old enough to be inconvenient, ugly, expensive to keep up, and without any charm whatsoever. He and his son, Fergus, had named it Crumbles in despair of ever having enough time to do more than hold it together with a bit of thatch for the roof one year, paint the next, and endless hope. Helen had spent a spangled fortnight there with Simon one early spring; she had never thought she could be so happy with so much mud about.

"I hear dear Webby got the consummate caning of all time this morning. Channing was a veritable Cheshire cat when he told me of it."

"Heavenly sound to wake up to, the little beast's screams. I must say good old mom upstairs didn't turn a hair."

"I gather the parents are self-protectively oblivious to him, from what I heard last night and this morning. It does sound as if they're writing 'Duet for Typewriter and Calculator' up there, does it bother you?"

"No, it's restful, listening to other people work. This place is a beehive of industriousness. D'you think I could learn to shuck peas or something?"

"Shell peas, shuck corn, my urban dunce. Go back to sleep for a bit. I'll bring our lunch in about one." He put a light kiss on her already closed eyes, straightened the quilt, and closed the door softly.

So softly that Helen, thinking he was still there, murmured drowsily into the pillow, "Have you ever heard of a kind of arthritis that has quick, stabbing pains? I always thought it a slow, duller, constant—her feet and ankles are so beautiful, not a bit swollen or gnarled, and her hands when she crumbled that—I wonder what—" Helen slept.

# CHAPTER II

Judah Carlson pulled at the edge of the blanket Katey had rolled herself in, uncovering one foot, which he began to tickle gently with a strong, grease-ingrained finger. She buried her head farther in the pillow, trying to avoid the light from the windows Judah had uncovered when he came in. "C'mon, Katey, it's noon. I broughtcha them things you wanted from the store."

Katey rolled over, sat up, pushed fine streamers of silver blond hair from her face, and yawned. Terrible crowd last night at the Black Griffon, she hadn't gotten home till three. Judah was recounting the events of his morning as he moved with familiarity among Alf Bemis's kitchen furnishings. "—So I got the garbage for the dump in the back of the truck; mostly jugs. They sure git down a lotta wine over to the big house, don't they? Old Tucker was asking me if they went up to Vermont to get it cheaper—nosey old cuss, always was—and I told him no, it all came right from Schmichael's. Ada's smart, ain't she, not to change the name of the store. Folks around here think Beemeadows is nutty enough without rocking the boat any further. Want an egg with your toast or anything?"

Katey pulled a T-shirt, which had spent the night on the floor, over her head as Judah put her breakfast on the seat of a chair by the bed. He sat at the foot, his hard, knotted mechanic's hands in swarthy contrast to the white skin of her feet as he rubbed them gently. The telephone rang, Katey reached for it.

"Yeah?—Yes, when?—All right." She lit a cigarette, sipped at the mug of coffee. "So how are things down at the Chetford Body and Fender Works?" she asked languidly.

"Aw, same as ever. Slow as molasses. Ada's always sellin' off my time to folks for odd jobs, like up here to Beemeadows, but to tell the truth there ain't enough at the garage to keep me busy all the time anyway and as long as she's willing to pump gas for me whilst I'm out, I don't care. Can get up here to see you, for one thing, and that's bettern' checking under hoods and wiping windshields any day. Wanna ride along to the dump with me? Nice day out."

Katey found a rubber mouse tangled in her blanket, tossed it across the floor to where her cat's other toys were, ate some toast. "I dunno. Say, where's Magnificat? Did you see her outside? She gets lost and eats the most awful things—she was choking on some mouse bones yesterday when I woke up."

"Nope, she wasn't out there when I come in. Probably chasing woodchucks again. Or hangin' around old Perce's kitchen hoping for a free feed. She's okay. Say, didja hear about that jeezly little kid Webby and what he did to them visitors up to the house?" Katey listened with half her attention, knowing she'd hear it all later in the day anyway.

"Rotten little snot," she commented as Judah gathered up her dishes and took them into the kitchen. "Did I tell you he found that patch of pot I planted last month and I caught him smoking some of it green? Sick as a dog. Serves him right. No, I don't want to go to the dump, I better go see where my cat is, for one thing."

"Aw, she'll be okay, K. Funny about that Webby, he's nice to your cat—loves to brush her and has a real gentle touch. Told me his ma won't let him have any pets at home." His slightly furrowed, fortyish, sunburned face looked beseechingly down at her, lying back on the pillows, staring at the ceiling. "I sure miss you nights, Katey. Come on, we've just got time for a nice old roll before the dump opens."

"Oh. Well, why not? I don't mind."

*

Channing and Webster sat baking in the afternoon sun in front of Carlson's garage, waiting for Judah. He had just rattled in with his truck, the back full of empty garbage cans, and had run into the little office to answer the telephone. Webster was perspiring heavily in his plaid madras Bermuda shorts, suede sneakers, and acrylic polo shirt; Channing, in his old white tennis shorts, cotton T-shirt, and bare feet, was equally hot but philosophical. Webster wanted to go in and beard Judah in his lair; Channing had waved a prohibitory finger. "Inner sanctum. Too crowded in there for three of us, for one thing, if you think you're hot out here. Besides, men around here like to do business standing up, for some reason, and preferably out of doors. You'll see."

"Positional power, so they can get away?" Webster's face shone with expertise.

"Very likely." Privately, Channing was thinking he should have kept his mind on the moment and not on the rest of the afternoon, and found a way to leave Webster back at the farm before coming down to see Judah. Hayward had no place in his self-appointed task of trying to help straighten out the problems Beemeadows was having with Chetford County's zoning board, and was making matters worse instead of better. Not that Channing had made much progress himself, but he knew that was only because of lack of time and application. As soon as he could, his name and technique would get them all a great deal further than Webster's forced bonhomie, which someone like Judah had seen through and mistrusted in a flash.

"Hey there, Channing, what can I do for you?" Judah leaned one arm, tattooed with a fouled anchor, on the door of Channing's little Fiat. "Louisa filled 'er up early this morning."

"Afternoon, Judah. Say, that tune-up you gave her was great, she's putt-putting along like a good girl now. No, I was hoping that was Tucker or Marshall on the phone and that the three of you've finally gotten a day set for our hearing with you. My schedule's getting a bit tight for the rest of the month."

"Yeah, Carlson, but even if Channing can't make it, I'll be here and I'm sure we can get it straightened out, fella." Webster leaned across the front seat and grinned at the mechanic, who was also one of Chetford's three zoning commissioners.

"Aw, Channing, I did talk to old Tucker and he's around, but Marshall's the sticker. He wants to put it off another month now. He's got an insurance case over to Pittsfield all of a sudden, first case he's had for a while, you know, he's like an old fire horse when the bell rings. Don't think we can all get together for you folks till Marshall's free."

"That's a shame, Judah—your decision's holding up some of our insurance, you know. If the statutes say all three commissioners must be present on a zoning hearing, we could get together in the evening, I'd think. The matter's not that complicated."

"Heck, Channing, we always *do* meet in the evening. Tucker ain't got nothing to do but hold up the hollyhocks, but I got the garage and Marshall still hangs out in his old office in Pittsfield every day anyway, retired or not. Nah, he said to tell you to wait a month and he'll have some time."

"Now listen, Carlson." Webster pulled a damp notebook out of his hip pocket. "As far as your being busy with the garage, I see your truck up at Katey's cabin most of the time to begin with." Judah's position at the car's window didn't

change by a hair, but Channing saw the sudden tension be-
trayed by the rippling of the tattoo on Judah's massive fore-
arm. Webster babbled on. "It says in the statutes there's a
limitation on the number of postponements a zoning hearing's allowed. From what I find in the record up at Beemeadows that's just about used up; you fellas are gonna have to
move it pretty soon or, as I see it, we'll be forced to apply to
the courts to get you to hold your hearing."

Channing laughed, moved the wheel idly. "Webster's got a
touch of the sun, Judah. No need for that if you're sure
Marshall's final about next month. Appreciate it if you'll keep
him to it."

"Well, sure, Channing, I'll lean on him, but if you ain't
here Ray or Louisa or Perce or Ada'd have to be there, one of
the co-owners, you know." He looked pointedly away from
Webster.

"Just so. Louisa has to be in the city once more, but one of
us'll be around and I'll do my best to be there myself. Okay,
Judah, thanks."

"Right." Judah gave the trunk of the Fiat a friendly thump
as he went around the back and into Schmichael's. Webster
puffed, letting out pent-up frustration, and let himself out of
the car and disappeared into the post office with a sheaf of
manila envelopes to be sent, registered and insured, to publishers and clients in New York.

Channing looked at the clock on the dashboard, seeing
weeks on the face instead of hours. The Haywards were a mis-
take, even the first week early in June without little Webby
had shown it. Nothing to do about it now except wait out the
short month they had left, and simply let any further interest
on the Haywards' part in entering Beemeadows slide. Louisa,
of course, bore the brunt of it now—he himself was away too
much to be more than mildly irritated. But with Louisa at the
main house so much, and Webster's need to use the telephone so frequently while she was working—"It seems *always*

when I'm adding up the books or trying to project next year's budget for road work or haying and all that," she'd sighed, acceptingly but tiredly, "and you know how I get with figures when I'm interrupted." Channing regretted seriously the casual invitation he'd tossed out in the spring. He'd see to it the summer ended gracefully, of course, since he'd be running into Sally from time to time in New York; her inept and obvious machinations to get his consultative position at the Bayard Foundation for Webster needed to be watched until the time came—around November, Channing thought—to get *that* scotched once and for all. It'd be like shooting fish in a barrel, of course, but the timing was important and he needed until Thanksgiving at least to be on ostensibly good terms with the Haywards.

Louisa must invite them up for Halloween—he himself would be in Denver then—that should keep things going just long enough. Damn it, this was a hell of a time for her to have rheumatism or lumbago or whatever, it put more of the routine errands on him than he wanted, such as this one, but driving was chancy for her. On top of it all, to take on finding a nursing home for one of those old servants—her nanny, that was it. Typical Anstruther loyalty, of course, and the lame old duck she'd been clucking over, running back and forth to New York, seemed to be getting settled. About time. At least she'd been taking the bus from Lee up and down, which left him the car for himself. One more trip, she'd said, next week. He'd have to put his foot down after that. The pain killers she was taking left her so tired and fuddled and—remote— sometimes when he needed her to edit or type a speech and especially to grade those dreary seminar papers this summer—

He eyed Judah's battered pick-up in the rearview mirror, unconsciously tautening the muscles of his stomach and jaw at Webster's very counterproductive crack to Judah about seeing the truck up at Katey's so often. Channing had been wary of Alf Bemis subletting his cabin to anyone; if he hadn't known how much Alf needed the money he would have voted against it altogether. As it was, he'd found Katey himself at Greenfield; she was quiet and hadn't brought swarms of kids around from Great Bedford, and Judah was actually more useful to the farm now that she was there. He kept to his garbage pick-up schedule for a change, and he and Ray were getting the new roof on the old woodshed finished while Judah waited for Katey to get her sleep in the mornings.

If anything, the girl was avoiding the community rather than intruding on it; he smiled again, remembering Webster's ill-concealed interest in her and the girl's quick rejection. Hayward was turning sour on her now, of course. She knew her own mind; one of his better students. He tapped his hand on the horn; Webster was taking an age in there and he had to get back and get rid of him, grab the hour he needed alone, and be in Pittsfield at four-thirty.

Too bad about Helen Bullock's broken foot last night, it'd be interesting, but more likely irritating, to have her around. She saw too much and probably said it—there'd always been an unedited "here it is" quality to her photography and writing. He'd paid attention to it when *Globe* was at its best and he was fooling around with photography himself. A very direct, flat-out woman. Not rude or ill-bred, but—undissimulating.

Perce's cousin, Bede, was a definite plus. Might be interesting to have him join that next Saturday Seminar Channing was holding at Greenfield. Turn it into a dialogue, clashes of interest in multinational industries versus civil rights in Africa, for instance. Bede knew his way around that one with one hand tied behind his back, after all the work he'd done on the Anglican Communion's African investments, as Channing did.

Webster slammed the door loudly and buckled both his seat belts, puffing again. "Don't you think we could have leaned a little harder on that Carlson fella, Channing? These yokels spin you along with the tourist season, haying season, hunting season—anything but work season."

"He'll come around, Web, don't worry." Channing started up the road toward Beemeadows. "Judah's on our side to begin with, of course—that's mostly Ada's doing, they get along like Laurel and Hardy, and I doubt Marshall cares much one side or another but simply wants his perks as a zoning commissioner. The retired lawyer syndrome. Tucker's the nut to crack, and since his son-in-law sells insurance and we're going to need a bit more, it's pretty much open and shut once I get over to Pittsfield later this afternoon and look the chap up. The word will filter straight to Tucker, the hearing'll be a formality."

"Well, hell, why's it all taking so long, then?"

"Ego trips. We're being made to cool our heels because we went ahead and built. Only way to get it done if we wanted to move in this spring, which we did. If we'd played the game their way and applied for zoning permission first, cap in hand so to speak, the pleasure of keeping an Adaams at heel for a season would have been irresistible. However, now it's built they're not going to make us tear it down. We'll simply be put through a draggy and possibly amusing session or two to disconvince them that the code of one dwelling per three acres isn't being violated by having Ada and Perce back to back in the chicken house. That's the gun they've loaded and the one we'll have to spike. Easy enough, especially now that the main house is only for guests from time to time and is officially an 'office.' Redraw the acreage—God knows there is enough, one hundred seventy-five acres—so a border of one runs directly through the dividing wall in the chicken house, or something. Fun and games in the country." He turned off the blacktop road into the gravel lane leading to the farm.

"Say, speaking of spiking guns, Chan, Sally wanted me to have a talk with you about Webby. We heard you paddled him this morning. We don't believe in corporal punishment, you know, for children." Webster mopped his forehead.

"That may be. I do know that Miss Bullock has a very corporal broken foot to show for Webby's unsupervised ingenuity. Afraid we're going to have to insist you and Sally give the boy some perimeters, Webster. It's been one thing after another since he was sent back from camp, mud pies in the cars, leaving lights on, letting woodchucks into the garden, toys all over the floor of the house, candy and gum wrappers on the lawn, jamming the typewriter in the office with bubble gum."

"Well, I know, I know. Dr. Blanford said that'd all be likely, aggression to postpone punishment he fears for failing at camp. I'll tell Sally how you feel and see what she says."

"Lord, what's that?" Channing turned into Beemeadows' entrance from the gravel road; Katey was standing in the middle of the drive, tears running down her face; Simon Bede was beside her, holding a strangely poised and stiff Magnificat in his arms. Channing stopped, got out.

"I'm sorry, but I get all sick to my stomach with dead things—I did love her—" Katey finished saying, turning to Channing. "Your friend here said he was up in the meadow where the blackberries are, you know, by the road to your house, and—"

Simon took over as the girl's sobs were muffled in her hair and hands. "Pity, she was a lovely thing. Mrs. Adaams had just shown me the thicket where the blackberry canes are and had started back to your house; the cat had been with her until then, but must have gone into the thicket after something. Poor thing must have tackled something a bit too rough for her, came screaming out past me, all hunched up, went on a few paces, and just dropped. No marks or bites I can feel." Simon's strong, square hands held the dead cat gently, still stroking the unfeeling, long silky fur. "Snakes?"

"God knows," Channing said, his arm around Katey. "Might be a copperhead or two from time to time. Webster, take the car and Simon on up for me, will you. Come on, Katey, inside, we'll bury her for you under the stump of the old elm, remember how she used to love to sit on that and wait for woodchucks?" Channing nodded over his shoulder to the men, steering Katey into her cabin. "That's a good place, nothing will get to her there."

"I knew I should have kept her inside—she *wasn't* used to the country—"

"Nonsense, child, she had a wonderful time right up until the last—" Channing shut the door of the cabin.

"I'll drop you with the car at the barn, you can find a shovel there or get Ray to do it." Webster was clearly going to have no part in burying a dead cat. He parked the car rather sloppily half in and half out of its stall, and hurried toward the house.

＊

Simon and Ray stood beside the little grave behind the barn. Simon had wrapped Magnificat in an old piece of terry cloth from the rag bag in the workroom, and then in a thick plastic utility bag. They laid her gently in the earth among the gnarled roots of the dead elm, and when the earth was piled back Ray had made a small cairn of stones to keep away predators and mark the spot for Katey. "Shame, such a pretty thing. Just like Katey in a way." Ray straightened up. "Enough of a kitten to be sweet and silly, but grown up enough to be gorgeous, and know it. Remember my daughter at that age."

Ray took their shovels back to the barn, and Simon began the pleasant ramble back up through the woods to the blackberry thicket where he had left the huge colander Perce had given him to fill.

Helen had been sound asleep, both codeine and pain hold-ing her deeply under, when he had looked in to see if she were hungry about twelve-thirty. He had left a quick sand-wich and glass of milk on the file cabinet by her watch and gone up to the Adaamses'. Not much of a task, Louisa had known exactly where Channing wanted the South American collection hung and in what pattern, it was only a question of a short stepladder on the hearth and a few hooks and nails. Magnificat had been prowling around, sniffing at the dried-out old basketwork, pouncing on feathers and beads; he and Louisa had laughed when she sneezed from the dust.

Extraordinarily odd, he thought as the level of purple-black fruit rose in the colander and the inevitable scratches of berry-picking increased on his hands and forearms. Louisa had carried the cat down the road with her until they had come to the berry thicket; she had left Simon on the far side, recom-mending the fruit farther down as riper, it got the full after-noon sun. He saw her, as he began picking, fondling the cat, then quickly put her down, shooing her toward the road down. Magnificat, incensed, had torn into the thicket in proud rejection. Louisa, walking slowly back up the road to her house, must have heard the poor beast tearing out the other side of the bushes, but she had continued to walk away, very slowly, the calm smocked back unruffled by those few scalp-raising rasping screeches of the dying cat.

At least, he mused, he didn't have to evade aspects of the accident with Helen, who loathed even the mention of snakes. He and Ray had found a splintered, bloody mass of bones and feathers firmly lodged in the cat's sad throat when Simon had tried to close its mouth before wrapping it up in its shroud. Poor thing, the bird's bones must have pierced an artery inside for her to die so quickly. No comfort to Katey to know, particularly, and Channing seemed to be on top of tak-ing care of her for the moment, at least.

*

Perce turned on the cold tap full force, letting the icy spring water hiss over the peck of fresh spinach Thelma had left on the back porch for dinner. Should be enough. He scanned a gargantuan platter of elegantly carved ham, a bowl of mustard and yogurt sauce, a saucepan of lightly scrubbed new potatoes waiting in their self-stained pinkish water, and an empty tart shell of restaurant proportions, the gigantic colander he'd given Simon next to it, full of fruit.

Perce pried off the top of a bottle of ale and stood, leaning against the kitchen doorjamb, watching Thelma and Bede in the distant garden, coping with Japanese beetles on the raspberry canes. Thelma's solution was to shake them off into jars full of water where they quite philosophically let themselves drown into a mass of something that looked like currant jam when the jar was full. Lots of the little buggers this year, but not many slugs so far.

The four o'clock sun gave the side porch, which he could see out of the edge of his eye, with its border of stock, delphinium, lilies and lawn and the vegetable garden beyond, the look of a particular Vuillard he wished he could own, the blue and green and hot purple shadows of chard, rhubarb, corn, lettuce, the first tomatoes like glowing pale orange lanterns. There was a lady in that painting, her blue smock and garden hat half hidden, that had always reminded him of Louisa, for some reason. Not that she'd ever had a chance to do any gardening, aside from getting in her first beloved white rose bushes this spring.

Nice chap, Simon, or seemed to be from the little Perce had seen of him. Brought out some brief tales on the front veranda yesterday when he'd arrived about the more distinguished Giffards, dead and alive, and recalled a complimentary remark or two by the archbishop after a conference at Adaams Park decades ago. Handsome, too, in a quiet way that didn't strike you at first but that for Perce's money more than held up to Channing's almost arrogant good looks. Bede's was a neater, more contained, yet warmer, mien, somehow. Pity about his friend's leg—he'd heard of her, of course, was reserving judgment on her since he had also heard her vocabulary when she fell into the hole, and it didn't seem quite —well, quite the thing for a lady.

She'd been quiet today, though, and didn't seem to need any looking after, thank heavens. Perce had a good day's work behind him, consequently. He took a drink of ale and chuckled to himself at the certain reaction to come of the affluent Muirs of Texas when he sent them their completed genealogy. That "A. Muir" they'd been so overweeningly proud of as the first Muir in the Colonies, and Virginia at that, had turned out to be "a Moor," indubitably black and the slave of a landowner. Perce's only regret was at the sure-to-be falling off of work from Texas; he'd get no recommendations from *them*. Nevertheless, their check would more than cover some luxuries, particularly the humidity-control system he was putting in his digs to keep his book bindings from splitting and warping. There was a quite adequate heating system which Perce and Ada shared, but he couldn't ask her to pay for half of something she didn't need. All she ever read was *The Racing Form* and *Weight Watchers*.

Louisa must have finished up for the day in the office; he saw her leaving by the side porch, carrying another of those dratted cartons. Channing passed her on the lane, waved, drove on. Perce saw he had a jacket on; Pittsfield, then. He'd undoubtedly keep his shoes off until he got there, though; the man loved going barefoot. Could have turned around and given Louisa a lift back up, wouldn't have taken more than a few minutes. Her day had probably begun at six, Channing's usual hour for breakfast, and wouldn't end until late—she'd said she had a stack of papers to go over for him for tomorrow.

Perce had found her this morning, about eleven or so it must have been, haggard to a point of alarm but managing a glow of pleasure as she knocked on his apartment door. She'd finally gotten the repairman for the huge Garland range in the kitchen, a treasure Channing had found in a restaurant close-out sale years ago. Perce loved it with his very soul; he'd been torn between getting Louisa to sit down in the kitchen armchair and have tea, elevenses, and fussing over the erratic broiler and warming oven with the repairman. His concern for Louisa had gotten the better of him, of course; he saw she drank the cup of tea and kept her legs up on a footstool. "Don't you want an aspirin, can I get your pills, whatever it is you take? Brandy?" She had her hands tightly clenched in the pockets of her old smock; her head, pressed back on the cushion of the chair, showed a profile like an agonized Nefertiti.

"No, no." Even a whisper seemed too strenuous. He'd tried not to flutter, that wouldn't help and the dismantling of the nether regions of the range was bad enough, noisy. He'd helped her up when she was ready, her hands on the arms of the chair thin claws, and led her out to the relative quiet of the porch and a lumpy but firm old rattan chaise. "Don't fret, Perce"—she'd smiled—"it comes and goes but mostly goes. I'll just sit a minute. Our hot-water heater's not working, brand new, too. It may be the cold showers aren't helping my dolors. Go keep an eye on the Garland—from the looks of that repairman he may very well reassemble it into a clothes wringer instead of a broiler."

Perce had been dragooned into lifting and holding things; when the repairs were finally finished, the time slip signed, and the repairman gotten rid of without the beer he was waiting for, Perce had slipped back to the porch. Louisa had gone, he saw her walking, apparently comfortable again, up the lane to her house, carrying some baskets whose colors blended with the faded flowers on her smock. No doubt to get Channing's lunch, which the king of the mountain would accept as his due. Louisa. He shook his head.

Dropping the empty ale bottle in the bin by the door, Perce sighed and went into the cool, dim kitchen, turned off the water, and idly stirred the soaking spinach with a long spoon. Three washings at least. He hooked up the drain and listened to the first water running out. His hand was numb just from that short immersion; the spring water all the houses used was deliriously cold; they scarcely ever needed ice cubes.

Have to do the floor, there was a midden around the stove of blacking, rust, old parts, burned matches. Fella had strewn all his junk around everywhere. He started the second water running, picked up the broom, and started by the armchair, sweeping up something crumpled in a ball by the skirted oak leg. Have to keep those tags that come on new parts or they cheat you. He smoothed it out, set the broom quietly in the corner, carried the paper to the better light of the window by the sink. It wasn't a tag after all, but an old photograph that must have fallen out of one of Louisa's pockets in her smock when she got up, pulling her hands out with that spasmlike jerk she had these days, especially when the weather was changing, when she was in pain.

Staring at the photograph with its quilted texture from being squeezed into a ball, he winced, forced himself to look at it again. Terry, in the new flowered dress she'd worn for the first time the last day of the United Nations Conference on Defining Aggression; he remembered her coming up from their cottage to the main lawn after luncheon when all the dignitaries were leaving, looking like a full-blown rose herself. He remembered thinking she'd been putting on weight and how it became her, but still he'd had to get her quickly downstairs into the kitchen for a cup of coffee; he'd noticed the stares of more than one of the delegates, whether at her décolletage or her tipsiness he couldn't say, but it was not the sort of memory Perce permitted people to take away from Adaams Park with them. Terry. Had he put the Park first too often for her? There had been so little he could do for her at all, except give her his name and his home and pretend he thought the increasingly frequent glasses of amber liquid were iced tea, as she said. She'd stopped bothering to kiss him a long time before, of course.

Ill-equipped. He had been ill-equipped. For people, for love, for Terry. She had never smiled at him the way she was smiling in the photograph. He peered at it closer, sucked in his breath. It was taken at night, on the famous widow's walk at the Park, the flash bulb pointing up the old gingerbread railings. He suddenly thought to wonder, and at almost the same instant knew, who had taken it. And left it, forgotten, all these years.

Over twenty-five years ago; the shutter had snapped, the negative seized the light and imprisoned it on its emulsion, recording Terry's lush young beauty and the desire in her eyes. She'd been found dead the next morning, fallen from somewhere off the upper stories of the house, sprawled in her new dress among the late summer flowers.

He felt a sudden torrent of ice water running down his seersucker trousers. The floor was awash, the spinach in the sink overflowing. He firmly turned off the tap, remembered where he was, that there was dinner to get. Pray God Louisa's increasingly frequent lapses of memory would encompass the existence of the photograph in a benign cocoon; denying its existence would be all Perce could do for her now.

He began mopping up the freezing cold water, wishing his brain were as numb and chilled as his hands. Why was that line from—what was it? *The Jew of Malta*, that was it—running through his head: ". . . committed fornication, but that was in another country, and besides, the wench is dead."

# CHAPTER III

"Simon, I have the feeling I'm living in the middle of a sampler. You know, one of those with 'Idle Hands Are the Devil's Workshop X X X Abigail Folger A.D. 1703' in cross-stitch, and then the border with scenes of rural life—" Helen looked up from her work on the veranda and waved a long pair of cropping scissors about. Perce, a battered Panama on his head even before the sun had fought through the sweeping trees of the eastern mountain, was taking a bucket of scraps and mash over to the barn for the chickens. Thelma, outside the garden enclosure for once, was stretching netting over the wealth of blueberry bushes that straggled up the meadow. Ada, Judah, and Ray were fussing over a bright red mowing machine in the distance; most of the hay had been cut the day before by the farmers' co-operative that owned the machine, but there was one last meadow behind the house to finish. And, as always, the rattle of typing came from the Haywards' workroom upstairs.

"I know it's early—sorry to wake you—" Channing was in the office, telephoning. "Have to be around eleven?—*that's* better—splendid." The grandfather clock in the living room struck eighty-thirty; almost simultaneously "Fur Elise" began to be thumped out on the old square piano in the living room. Webby, too, had his tasks.

The Adaamses' dark blue Fiat swept down the lane from their house, stopped by the front veranda. Louisa got out, smiling, in a neat linen city dress and jacket, pumps, a handbag. Her heavy black hair was pulled up in a neat twist, the white plume very handsome against her dark skin, which for once had good color. "We're dropping you at the store, Simon? It's going to be dreadfully hot in the city, terrible day to have to go. Boston'll probably be worse than New York, though. Poor Channing. Helen, I can't tell you how dear you are to do all that pasting for me—I'd love to myself, but—"

"Louisa, I have no domestic accomplishments whatsoever, this is all I can do, and you did all the scut work anyway, sorting and dating them all. I've nothing else to do, especially since Simon's abandoning me this morning. Isn't it a gas out there?"

They all looked at the mowing machine; Ada was now mounted on the seat, her enthusiasm and pride evident even across the long meadow. Louisa laughed. "Such a dear—she and Judah have a running battle going about who's the better driver, you know, so he dared her yesterday to try out the mower—it's now or never since the co-op's taking it on across county tomorrow."

"So she said." Simon shoved his feet into a pair of moccasins, stood up. "Fun for me to keep store this morning; I don't know how I'll do with Judah's gas pumps but he doesn't seem to be nervous."

"Come off it, Simon, you know perfectly well you ran the socks off your tank all across North Africa during the war; if you can fill the tank of a tank you can manage the odd Pinto. Ada was sick with jealousy, by the way, about the tank corps."

"Mmmm. Wish I could find her one around here. Well, I daresay the bacon-slicing machine will get me first after all."

"What took you so long, Louisa?" Channing came bursting out, tucking his watch into his vest pocket, urbane, gray-suited, wearing a beautifully polished pair of shoes for once. "You forgot *again* about ordering that new coil for the hot-water heater, I left a note for Ray on the blackboard, at least I can depend on *him*. Come along, we'll be late and you'll miss your bus." He headed down to the car. Simon left a kiss on the top of Helen's head and squeezed into the back seat beside two suitcases.

"Good-bye, Helen. So glad you can finally walk without those crutches—" Louisa was looking about her very slowly, her mind far away from Helen's progress with either photographs or mending bones. She touched a pillar of the veranda very softly, her long fingers giving a caress to the flaking old paint. Channing called to her to hurry. She pulled herself back to the moment, gave a last smile to Helen, and went down to the car.

"Shall I drive, dear?"

"Don't be an utter ass, Louisa, get in." Channing shoved her into the passenger's seat, slammed the door, and ran around to the other side. Simon made a droll face from the rear window as the little car scooted off.

Sitting back an hour later, Helen lit a cigarette and drained the last drops of now cold coffee from the mug on the table. Glorious day—Ada was making enormous swaths in the hayfield, getting the hang of it now, cutting long straight paths in smooth rows of fallen grass. Ray, mopping his forehead, left the two of them to it and headed down the field toward the barn, shaking his head at Judah, who was striding along beside the machine, nattering visibly if inaudibly at Ada's problems with the gears.

"Nice-looking couple, aren't they?" Perce set down a fresh pot of coffee on the table beside her, leaned for a moment on the veranda railing. "We all hoped their affinity would ripen, Ada and Judah, but then Katey came along—"

"Really? As a matter of fact, that would have been very nice, wouldn't it?"

"Most appropriate. Would have, however. Nothing to blind a man to his downfall like a pretty face. Perhaps, in the autumn—Hum. Very kind of Simon to take the store for Ada this morning. Hum. Wanted to say for myself, although I'm sure Louisa has already done so for the community, how pleasant it is to have you both here, Miss Bullock. At my age a relation, however distant, is always of interest, and in this case a distinct pleasure."

"Why, thank you, Perce. Yes, Simon's a dandy. A flower in the world's buttonhole, I always think." The compliment he had paid Simon was almost killing the old gent, Helen thought, saddened at his rustiness. Nice of him to make the effort.

"I never had much opportunity to know the English side of my family; up until now I thought it just as well, but I see I was wrong."

"I think Simon feels the same way about his American connections—glad his Aunt Priscilla got the two of you together finally. Oh, all these snapshots reminded him of a terribly funny story about a cousin you have in common in England, I can't remember which one but the guy must be younger than Simon, he was at Eton during the war—"

"Ah? Let me see, who would that be—"

"Simon'll tell you later. But apparently the kid was a camera nut at the time, and toward the end of the war one of those ghastly buzz bombs or rockets fell near enough to the school to break most of the glass in the chapel. It was early in the morning and the kid jumped out of bed, grabbed his Brownie or whatever, and went rushing down to photograph the damage. He found the school chaplain dancing gleefully up and down on the remnants of the old glass in the aisles calling out, 'Come along, lad, come along, help me smash it to smithereens so it can *never* be restored!' Apparently the glass was not only dreadfully ancient and historic but dreadfully, dreadfully hideous and the chaplain had wanted to get rid of it for years!"

"Ha! And so it was. So it was. Remember it well from choir-exchange tours with Charterhouse. Well. Must get Simon over to our little church in Otis—quite a gem, a gem. Clear glass, of course."

"I'm sure he'd love it, but we're feeling a bit like cuckoos who've landed in your nest or something—you only expected us for a cup of tea four days ago; I'm in very portable shape now—"

Perce held up his hand. "Four days and yet four more and again four more, we all hope. I'll speak to Simon, you mustn't think of leaving yet. So many lovely excursions to make from here."

He took Helen's sticky brown hand in his old freckled one with a thin, gold signet ring on his little finger, bent over it, and gave it the most gentlemanly kiss possible. "Now you must excuse me, an old colleague in New York needs verification on a collateral branch of a family I happen to specialize in." He made what was almost a bow and shuffled off around the porch, leaving Helen warmed and amazed and feeling a bit like a rural mailbox by the side of the road that Perce had used to leave a message in for Simon. He'd never unbend enough to be so friendly to his face.

She stumped carefully into the house, went through the dark little office into the bedroom, and took the folder of prints and negatives from the wicker rocker; Louisa had forgotten them. Drat, she hadn't dated them or even said if she wanted them in the book—Helen flipped through; she could figure out the chronology herself, but decided to leave two blank pages in case she did want them in, put the folder on the window sill, and went back out to the veranda.

Webby had given up on the piano and was batting a tennis ball against the side of the barn, puffing with the exertion. Poor kid, an awful lot of his mischief must be sheer boredom, like his overeating. One day he'd taken all the eggs from the barn and hard-boiled them, and then put them back in the nests for Perce to find. Really, it was funny, but iniquitous too. Sad. Well, she thought, everyone had their season in life, and childhood wasn't Webby's. He'd come into his own later on, perhaps, if the world let him *live*. Helen poured a fresh

cup of coffee and set back to work, reaching for a fresh
album.

\*

"So he finally got to you?" Simon tickled the back of
Helen's knee with a spear of grass.

"What? Hello, darling. What got to me?" Helen was
facedown, half asleep on an old quilt spread out on the lawn.
She'd finished the last album just before noon, and feeling either very overdressed or underdressed—a bikini and a plaster
cast somehow didn't quite go together—had fallen asleep in
the clear bright sun.

"Webby, I surmise. He's been at you for days to let him
write something on your cast, hasn't he?"

Helen sat up, twisting her head around and glaring at the
red heart on the back of her cast, drawn with a felt-tip pen,
and the rudely scrawled "C screws C" inside it. "Oh, the little
bastard. He must have snuck up when I was asleep. I'll kill
him."

"Don't. They'll ask me to preside at the funeral and I'd
find it difficult to do it with any seemly show of charity or
regret. What d'you think he means, 'C screws C'?"

"You know perfectly well—it's who, I wonder? Channing's
the only C around, isn't he? Think it'll scrape off? It was
such a *pretty* cast, all clean and country pure."

"I'll put sticking plaster around it, there's some in our loo.
Had lunch? How're the archives?"

"Not yet, and all finished. What time is it, anyway?"

"One-thirty or so—Ada came down covered with hayseed
and glory and happy as a sandboy. Took back her store and
sent me up to look after you with apologies for being late."
The mowing machine had disappeared; the meadows lay flat
and sparkling.

"You walk back up, then?"

"Mmm. Nice stroll. Missed you. Hope Louisa caught her bus; Channing barely stopped long enough for me to fling myself out and they went roaring on. Pity to waste the day on wheels, bus or car." He lay back and kicked off his moccasins. "Shall I go native and take to bare feet and bathers like Channing?"

"Hmmm. Why not just a short kilt. Be original."

"I shall." He sat up abruptly. "I shall shortly proceed to the kitchen and make us highly original sandwiches. I brought the innards of them back with me. As well as your *Times*, with the puzzle unworked, bug spray, foul cigarettes, and shampoo."

"Goody. Was it fun, the store?"

"Rather, yes. Ada's given me a telephone call to make for her. Her nephew in New York isn't reachable until ten and there was a hot thing called Curtsey in the ninth at Aqueduct she wanted ten on."

"Simon, don't pretend to me you understand a word of what you're saying."

"Of course not, but I *sound* splendid, don't I? Don't stick a pin in my balloon, it was jolly good fun and quite legal. Her nephew nips into the local Off-Track Betting office on his lunch hour and places Ada's wagers for her for five per cent of the winnings. Just as I was talking to the lad an old gaffer came in and was most disapproving. Said he'd heard I was 'the mackerel snapper priest up to that Beemeadows' and his name was Tucker. We had a long, beer-soaked discussion about the vast unbridgeable *chasms* between Rome and Canterbury—"

"Simon! After your last twenty years working to bring them together? What a *liar* you are!"

"Yes, it was glorious! But you know how the word 'priest' is a horror to fundamentalists. Had to do what I could. I threw in a bag of potato crisps."

"Chips."

"Chips, and we moved on to the troublesome business among the local busybodies about Ada's love for the horses. They all approve of her thoroughly by this time, but a few don't quite approve of gambling."

"Except poker, pin-ball machines, horseshoes, canasta parties, bingo, door prizes at the local V.F.W. dances, and secret dreams of a week in Vegas."

"Quite. Then we proceeded to life at Beemeadows generally; I gather the farm's on a sticky wicket with the zoning commission. Channing has been precipitous and Webster's gotten everyone's goat."

"And true to form you smoothed it all out, hmm? With one hand tied behind your back?"

"Not a bit of it. I broached another hogshead of beer, dispensed a free round of dried beef jerky, assured him I'd seen no sign of anything but pleasantly middle-class, middle-aged behavior, and sent the old chap out with a sodium and alcohol level in his system that'll keep his glands busy for days."

"Simon, you're terrible. After that guzzle I don't see how you can be hungry, but I am."

"Oh, I paced myself, I assure you." He picked up the groceries. "Attend my return here, wench."

"Hey, bring the adhesive tape out when you come," Helen called after him, suddenly very hungry. She lay on her back, amazed at the sky. A shadow fell across her outstretched arm. "Hi, Katey."

The girl looked like a dandelion, her green petal-skirted dress settling around her as she sat down on the grass, the long golden hair pinned up softly around her face. Pretty to see a dress, we all wear jeans and things too much, Helen thought. "If you're hungry Simon's in the kitchen fixing sandwiches—give him a holler and he'll do one for you too."

"No, I've just eaten, thanks." She was nibbling on a spear of wild onion or garlic, staring out at the shorn meadows absently, one smooth hand, childlike still in its purity and the last faint remnant of baby fat padding the skin, smoothing the hem of her skirt, splotchy with dust. A branch of white roses lay in her lap.

"Awfully sorry about your cat, Katey. Had you had her long?"

"About a year, since she was a kitten. I've just been sitting by her grave. I was afraid something might happen to her in the country; she was an indoor cat, you know, but it seemed mean to keep her shut up, she loved to go out exploring—"

"Yeah, I know. But at least she went quick, not mangled or hit by a car and lying for hours in a ditch or anything."

"I guess so. Well, I'd better get home, I'm getting burned." The top of her sundress barely existed except for a few complex straps and a minimal bib. "I can't take the sun, I just get red and peel. Hope your foot's better."

"Much, thanks." Katey rose, a powder of dust from her skirt settling on Helen's brown arm, and the scent of the flowers piercingly sweet. "Simon and I thought we'd try the Black Griffon for dinner tomorrow or the next night; give Perce two less to feed now that Louisa and Channing are gone too."

"Better wait—there's a group there this week that'll tear your ear drums out, unless you like loud rock."

"God, no. Thanks for the tip. See you."

*

Helen finished the wreath of dandelions she'd been stringing together and placed it on Simon's balding pate. "Here, this'll keep you from getting too sunburned."

"Aha! Eliot Lovborg shall come with vine leaves in his hair!" Simon put the ice bucket full of beer and mugs beside Helen, the stems of the dandelions sticking out, making him look a bit more like a stuffed scarecrow than Pan or Bacchus.

"Oh, lovely, do make me one too." Thelma came down from the garden, a dishpan full of tiny zucchini under her arm, and sank down on the quilt. "I do wish Ray'd stop puttering and come have a beer with us. He's been meaning to reupholster that chair for eighteen months and it doesn't have to be today." They waved at him as he pushed a dilapidated armchair in a wheelbarrow into the barn. "Glorious day, isn't it?"

How nice to be silly, Simon thought. Here we all are, bedecked with dandelions, Helen better, cold beer, slugs and beetles the only asps in Eden. He had helped Ray set up a purple martin house and unpack two beeehives in the hours after lunch; the man was apparently indefatigable but Simon felt now he'd done his own stint for the day, particularly since he had noticed the Haywards ignored their self-assigned task of after-dinner clean-up. Simon had taken to seconding Ada, who quietly and matter-of-factly stacked and rinsed dishes, loaded the dishwasher, and, quite forgivably in Simon's eyes, tended to brush crumbs onto the Haywards' laps while wiping the table.

"—I confess I didn't stop him. He didn't see me, I was hunkered down in the chard and rhubarb and there he was, felony in his heart as usual. Too funny for words. He nipped the jar open and got a finger in, and started licking it—well, they *do* look like jam, the beetles, all squished in there. The sheer fury!" Thelma was speaking of Webby, obviously. "Thank heavens they were dead; he threw the jar as far as he could—which isn't far—I'll have to get back and pick up the glass in a minute. Hope he didn't hear me laughing, he'd figure out a revenge I could do without."

Helen agreed, silently remembering the scribbling on her cast; Simon had taped it over when he brought their sandwiches out but she still felt it, which was silly, but she did.

"I hope Louisa rested on the bus this morning; it must have been dreadful in New York all day but I should think she'd be out on Long Island by now. She's going to stay with the old lady for a few days to get her settled in; perhaps that'll be a rest in itself for her. Did you really finish the scrapbooks?"

"Yep, it was fun. At the moment I feel like the world's greatest living authority on the life and times of Mr. and Mrs. Channing Adaams III. Interesting for me, a mini-history of home photography and journalism right there. I even found one of my own snipped from *Globe*. Nice and yellowing at the corners, just like me. God, I'd forgotten I went back so far! Channing's just ten years older than I am, but he sure doesn't look it."

"Oh, of course, you'd know all about the photography, how silly of me. Did you get nostalgic about the clothes? Remember the shoulder pads in the forties, and no stockings to be had during the war? I remember we used leg make-up and drew a fake 'seam' down the backs of our legs with eyebrow pencil. Never worked, smudged."

"Never. And peplums! To say nothing of shoe rationing. Simon, I think you're being hailed from the barn—at least you won't have to listen to secrets from the harem."

He groaned, set down his beer, and meandered across to where Ray was propping up a heavy stepladder, intending to reglaze one of the barn's high old windows. The two women watched, Thelma shaking her head and loosening unintentionally not only her own thick bun of rusty hair but the wreath Helen had put together for her. "Honestly, Ray's an addict, never stops. If Simon has any sense he'll tell him there's beer over here—that works sometimes. Simon's so nice, Helen. Silly of me, but I didn't know priests retired, exactly."

"Sure, just like the grown-ups. Well, in a sense, maybe not —'Thou art a priest forever, after the Order of Melchizedek.' But Simon's had twenty-five hot and heavy years of Anglican politics, and I think he's waiting just now to see if he really is retired or just on a long, long sabbatical. We're a bit in the same boat, me with *Globe* folding up and Simon with a new order at Lambeth. Maybe it's time to shift gears and find new directions. I don't know."

"I see. Shame about *Globe*. I was going through some old ones in the barn the other day—all mice-eaten, alas. They were from the forties."

"Hey, that reminds me. Didn't peplums go out in the forties or did they? There's a negative in the house of Perce's wife Terry; she's wearing a flowered dress and it's either got a pretty clumsy peplum or she was a bit preggers, maybe not, though. Everybody's ten pounds beamier on film, especially in big splashy-print dresses."

"I think she was, Helen—it wasn't brought out at the time she died—only four months or so. I only learned of it years later from Louisa." Thelma squinted up at a flock of birds trying to do battle with the netting on the just-ripening blueberries. "Perce must have been so happy, you can imagine. None of us had ever thought he'd marry, much less have a child. Terry was a little—ordinary—but so pretty and fun-loving. They were only married three years. Sad."

"How did she die? The obit was pretty—veiled. I know 'unexpectedly' used to mean suicide and 'after a long illness' cancer, but this just said 'a tragic accident.'"

"Talking about Terry?" Sally loomed behind them; for once she hadn't slammed the screen door when she came out of the house. "She fell off the widow's walk at Adaams Park sometime during the night, they didn't find her until the next morning of course, but she'd been up there with some guy, drinking, one of the gardeners, probably. Well, Thelma, don't look down your nose, she *was* a lush and we all knew it. Don't forget I was *there* that week—remember it like yesterday, one of my first jobs with Dreiser, the big UN conference, very important to me. When the conference ended after lunch that day Terry came wandering around the driveway in a new flowered dress cut down to the navel, tight as a tick.

*And* giving the glad eye to just about anything in pants—Perce came around and got her away, but not before everyone had noticed. Can't really blame her—she told me Perce was all washed up in that department for good. Anyway, it was all hushed up, her being drunk when she fell and so on. Marguerite and Channing saw to that, of course. No real loss to Perce when you look at it intelligently; she'd have gone on the same way if she'd lived, and ended up plastered on the front page of a newspaper in some sort of scandal even the mighty Adaamses couldn't hush up. D'you know if they left their house unlocked, by the way? I told Channing I needed his Foundation Directory while he was away. I got the keys from the office just in case."

Thelma, chewing on a piece of grass, looked wearily disgusted as Sally stood up, brushed off her grubby mattress-ticking tent dress, and strode on suede earth shoes, her huge utility basket of a handbag swinging from her arm, up the lane toward the Adaamses'. Webby came darting out of the barn, running after her, calling, "Hey, Sally, wait up, wait up for me!"

\*

"Woman, did you pinch my upholstery tacks? I saw you out in the garden hammering away at something." Ray and Simon, the window reglazed, addressed themselves to the beer bucket in the late afternoon light. Simon winked at Helen.

"I did not. I was re-enforcing the chicken wire where it's fastened to the posts and used brads, not tacks." Thelma gathered together the pieces of the broken beetle jar she'd collected and wrapped them in the want ad section of Helen's *Times*. "Trade you your tack hammer for my beer, though." She pulled the small tool sheepishly from her gardening apron.

"Humph. Then where the hell are my tacks? Got 'em for that chair a couple of days ago and they were right there on the workbench yesterday." He took another swig of Thelma's beer. "Thelma, Helen, is the perfect woman in all respects. Last Christmas I gave her her very own screwdriver for stirring paint, and not only does she use it for that but leaves mine alone now. We have an ideal marriage."

"You think two of everything is the answer? You may be right." Thelma laughed at him, taking back her beer. "What a marvelous smell." Perce had slipped from the chicken house to the kitchen earlier; something involving butter and onions was now cooking. Ada zoomed up the drive, swinging her car into the back of the barn after a friendly wave and beep on the horn. "Oh, dear, it must be way after five. . . . I'd better get these zucchini to Perce." Thelma started to get up but Simon stopped her. "Let me, Thelma, my turn to set the table in any event."

"Well, I accept. Nice out here." She leaned back against Ray; Helen pulled on a shirt against the cool. A woodchuck came out from behind a boulder, looking as if he had aspirations to run for the Presidency.

"Hadn't locked up after all." Sally swept up, a ponderous tome weighing down her basket. "And Webby deserted me halfway up there; the one time I needed him—he could have carried this back, weighs a ton. Anybody know where Webster is? Now he can get at addressing the envelopes. Oh, *there* you are, Webby—where's your father?"

Webby's rough-thatched doughy face appeared coming up the cellar steps. "Down there doin' the laundry," he puffed, running up to his mother, pulling at her skirt.

"Don't *tug*. Well, I'll put this down by the kiln for Channing when he gets back—Webby, don't *drag* on me so. Laundry, for heavens sakes! My god, it's hot as a kiln itself in that workroom of Channing's when it's all closed up—" She strode off to the cellar steps, digging out a piece of pottery from un-

derneath the directory, Webby still clinging to her. "Webster!" she called.

The silence wasn't as much fun as it had been. "Why is the kiln here in the house if Channing's the only one who uses it?" Helen asked, beginning to gather the afternoon's toys in a bundle.

"Gas." Ray lit his pipe. "Their house is all electric, stove, heat, and all, and with gas you can get up to cone nine on a kiln; gives you dishwasher-proof *and* stoneware."

"Think Ada'd come over for a beer, honey?" Thelma was draining the mugs onto the grass.

"You'd have to wait; you know how she is—near six now and she's gotta call New York to get the results from the track or she'll bust a gusset wondering what nag came in first. Great gal. Sky's changing," he said as he got up with a creak of his knees. "A weather breeder, I'd say."

# CHAPTER IV

Three days of Berkshire rain. Ray had been right. Helen managed the front seat of the car, braced with mildewed porch cushions and old army blankets for comfort during the day, and brandy at night. "Don't tut—if you hadn't promised Channing to meet him at Greenfield Saturday for his dratted seminar we could take off now and go on over to the Adirondacks. I suppose you're loving this drizzle, though. Very English." She pulled at Simon's earlobe; actually, it was rather fun mooching about the countryside.

Simon found an ancient golfing sweater and a handsome new tweed suit for five dollars in the Pittsfield thrift shop; they returned Helen's no longer needed crutches to the hospital, replaced Ray's upholstery tacks and a foot-long list of other necessaries at the hardware store; Simon bought Helen a bright red plastic garbage strainer for her apartment as a present. They found the plumber, ordered a new heating element for the Adaamses' hot-water heater, waving the warranty in his face. Helen found a blue glass pitcher with a white sailboat on it at the Goodwill; it cost a scandalous sum but she sent it to a dear pair of antique old ladies in Michigan. They'd had its exact duplicate for as long as Helen could remember and their house had burned to the ground last summer.

They sat in Miss Betty's coffee shop in Williamstown, eating far too many doughnuts and writing silly postcards bought at the Clarke Museum. "Don't you think there's something of Channing in this?" Helen tossed a print of the famous Bougereaux satyr surrounded by nymphs to Simon. "Don't snort—there *is*—not in coloring or looks, but in that air of 'it's all due me' sort of attitude." The swarthy satyr, wallowing in a wreath of pink-fleshed seducers a little less hefty than Rubens but still no Twiggies, did have that air of celestial confidence in himself, Simon conceded.

One day they cocked their snoot at old Tucker in Chetford and crossed into Vermont, returning to Beemeadows with a case of assorted liquors for the community at vastly lower Vermont prices, promising Ada to smuggle the empties out of state when they left. Simon presented Perce with a magnificent black-waxed wheel of Vermont cheese, challenging him to a soufflé contest.

They visited the Shaker Village nearby, had the car greased and the oil changed by Judah.

Still, three days of rain. Helen was glad of Simon's internal furnace at night, buttress against the damp sheets, and vowed their farewell present to Beemeadows would be an electric blanket for the guest room.

Friday morning Simon gathered a few books Channing had left for him, paper and pencil, and retired to the silo of the barn. Channing had turned it into a meditation platform, reachable by a long ladder to the top, when he was "into" TM and Eastern religions a few years ago. They were due to meet tomorrow morning for the Saturday Seminar; Simon felt anything he'd learned or known about African politics and investments needed considerable brushing up if he was to do credit to the occasion.

The living room had been taken over by Webby, struggling still with Beethoven. What had seemed to Simon an imposed task for the child, who played so very badly and with so little talent or musicality, had turned out to be Webby's choice. Sally had dismissed it with a shrug at dinner one night. "Oh, he taught himself, I don't know how, said he wanted lessons but Dr. Blanford's afraid he'd just use them as an escape mechanism, so many artists do to avoid their *real* problems. So I don't encourage his playing and we haven't a piano at home." The child had perseverance, Simon thought, remembering the score; "Für Elise" was easy, but not that easy, especially if one had no teacher.

Helen, feeling tired and rusted, opted for a morning in bed with the heating pad on her thigh. She'd read everything that looked appealing on the ground floor; what was left was terribly high-minded and serious. What she really wanted was some really good trash, or pornography, or *The Wind in the Willows*. Idly, she opened the drawer to the file cabinet by the bed. Folders, folders, folders. Not, she groaned, more photographs—she'd just about had the paste-pot bit. No, just letters—some from Channing's mother, others from Louisa to Channing, replies—fascinating! Helen shamelessly snuggled down, pulled the quilt up around her, oblivious to the dripping lilac tree outside and the damp that throbbed in her foot, and began to read.

*

Not so terribly fascinating after all, except for Marguerite's ill-scrawled tantrums about things from time to time—one self-defensive attack on Louisa for not having children and Channing's mumps when he was a child having been given the best medical care money could buy even though they were on a ship; one about her jewelry insurance premiums and no, she would not put it all in the bank, she wore it all the time even in bed, and it was perhaps thoughtful of Channing to have brought up those two South American strings of dead bones and shells from Louisa but that was more Terry's style and next time she'd much rather have something specifically for *her*, she'd heard the opals and emeralds down there were rather good. And Channing must do something about that dreadful little Perceval and the Park's board of governors; they were being quite difficult to her maid and nurses and it was an almost insuperable job in the first place to find anyone to look after her in her old age, a job Louisa should be doing if she had any sense of family—

Now this was interesting—Helen pulled out a small newspaper clipping, scarcely an inch long, stapled to a sheet of ruled paper on which there was a note written in the old Palmer method handwriting; an accountant, surely, the margins were so tidy as well. The little obituary announced the peaceful passing of Miss Pearl Rourke, age ninety-three, survived by her nephew and his wife, Mr. and Mrs. Herman Rourke, with whom she had made her home for the last twenty years. The note dated four years ago, was to Louisa, Dear Mrs. Adaams, thanking her for the wreath she had sent and enclosing two pictures of his aunt and Mrs. Adaams that Aunt Pearl had kept by her bed until the end, and that he and Mrs. Rourke thought Mrs. Adaams might like to have as a souvenir. Helen dug deeper in the file, found two brittle old pictures, both of a blue-caped, white-capped nurse holding a baby drowning in lace. Louisa? All babies looked much alike to Helen, particularly when squinting into the sun, but it said so in the letter. She must have had more than one nanny, then—very likely, really, if Anstruther had moved about as much as Helen had always heard he did.

She put the file back, yawned. Her watch said twelve; she needed a shower. She unplugged the heating pad and pulled a plastic garbage bag over her cast, wrapping it tight at the top with waterproof electrician's tape, and clumped into the bathroom. Simon would be down for lunch soon.

*

"—not there at Greenfield?" Why was it possible for Webster Hayward's *voice* to sound acrylic, she wondered as she pulled on a pair of jeans and a sweat shirt. Webster was quacking into the phone in the office next door. "Well, I don't understand. He left here Tuesday morning to go to Boston for the Teaparty Trust meeting and some other business over in Boston and at Paul Revere; it says on the calendar here he'll be at Greenfield all day today for the summer faculty meeting. One of the guests here is driving over tomorrow morning for Channing's Saturday Seminar—You have tried Boston?—Well, let me see—Give me your number and I'll ask around here—No, Mrs. Adaams is down in New York and won't be back for another day or so—Yes, yes, I'll call back as soon as I find out anything."

Webster scurried out of the office, calling for Sally and ringing the brass dinner bell out the back porch toward the barn, bustled back into the office, called the Russells, Perce. The quiet morning vanished in squishing shoes and dripping umbrellas on the veranda, questions and answers in the living room, office. Helen left the plastic bag over her cast and went out to the barn, called Simon down from the silo where he'd fallen asleep. Now he was leaning on the piano in the living room, talking to Ray. "No, not tonight, I was going to drive over quite early tomorrow morning—we'd arranged to meet at the Student Center at nine."

Webster came in from the office, sweating even in the chill, damp air. Helen glanced ruefully at the black, empty fireplace. "I got hold of the Teaparty Trust fella—says Channing didn't show up for the meeting Tuesday afternoon, but he wasn't surprised since in the summer only the old geezers with nothing better to do are in town and the young ones never are there. But that's not like Channing, even so."

"No, it's not," Perce clucked. "That's an extremely historic and important responsibility, the Teaparty—"

"Anybody got hold of Louisa yet?"

"I'm trying to find the number of the nursing home she was taking her nanny to; does anybody remember exactly where on Long Island it was?" Sally, her hair in rollers, stuck her head outside the office door. "Wouldn't the police have called here if there'd been an accident? I'm sure they would have." Thelma took a pair of slip-joint pliers Ray was fiddling with and put them on the coffee table. "Webby, if you want to play marbles that chalk won't hurt the dining-room rug and we won't trip on them in here—bring all your things, those pick-up sticks and your jacks too, dear—" She herded the boy into the dining room.

Simon and Ray were putting their slickers on; Helen found a mackintosh and let Simon help her thunk down into the back seat of Ray's car. The rain was softening to mist now; they swayed up the lane to the Adaamses', through the woods, an orchard, a new meadow, the jutting outcrops of rocks glistening dark against the green grass. Wouldn't it be a gas, Helen thought, if Channing were off in some hot pillow joint with somebody? Not likely, he'd cover his tracks too well, and besides, three whole days? And he certainly wouldn't put a bit of fluff before his trusts and boards and seminars and lectures, particularly tomorrow's dialogue with Simon. Kidnaped? There were all those people, businessmen, in South America. Not likely either. She couldn't see the Bayard Foundation or Greenfield College or any of his old bailiwicks ransoming him from a motel in Middletown, for instance. She almost giggled at the thought. But where the hell could he be?

Ray swung up into the driveway in front of a small, low-slung house facing the meadow, Louisa's roses heavy with rain around the front door, the foundation plantings adjusting to the shade of the thick woods as they wound around the back of the house into laurels, ferns, rhododendrons. When Ray shut off his engine, she could hear the low chuckle of the stream behind the house, swollen with three days of rain, spilling down the mountainside.

Simon pulled her out of the back seat, absent-mindedly put a piece of left-over slate under a dribbling downspout. The

rain had washed a small gully between the rose bushes. Nice
façade to the house, Helen thought, peaceful.

"Simon, Channing's car is here. In the carport around the
side." Ray came squishing back, the hood of his slicker down
his back. "His suitcase is on the back seat."

"Louisa's?"

"No, just his."

Sally had left the front door unlocked behind her when she
left after borrowing the directory; Simon picked up the ring
of a large and beautiful brass copy of the sanctuary knocker at
Durham Cathedral and let it drop, knocked again, called out.
Wiping their feet on a grass mat, they went into the foyer,
the living room. No answer. Damp and musty smelling, but
nice. Grasscloth walls, hemp rugs, white birch logs in the
fireplace; over it Channing's collection of South American
baskets, spears, flutes, masks. Louisa was right, it was a superb
collection and looked perfect there.

Twin beds in the bedroom, neatly made, bathroom with a
rumpled towel. A man's suit was neatly hung over the back of
a side chair in the bedroom, shoes and socks and underwear
folded precisely. Ray looked in the small kitchen. Empty
glasses, cups, plates rinsed and stacked neatly in a dish
drainer, an empty wine bottle in the garbage can. The little
room reeked of a heel of salami left out on the counter and a
wedge of that dreadful cheese Channing had brought down
for Simon and Helen to try one night—it tasted exactly like
what Helen thought a rotten cow's udder would, she'd
thought. The smell alone—

She went past them into Channing's workroom. Simon had
seen it and told her of it on a sunny day; now it was gray,
damp, a window behind his desk chair open, letting the wet
air in, but in spite of all, it was one of the most beautiful
rooms Helen had ever seen. Everything in it was the color of
tree bark: the leather couch, stained desk, and wall of file
cupboards, wooden mullions of the three nonreflecting glass

window walls, one with a door leading out onto the deck, the indoor-outdoor carpeting running straight out from the room itself onto the deck in a long uninterrupted rectangle of taupe with a faint tinge of lichen green. Must have been specially dyed for him, not a hint of the usual Howard Johnson colors one usually found in synthetic carpeting. An electric potter's wheel in a glass corner, facing trees and stream, its stool tilted back, leaning against the glass wall.

Simon looked at the desk with its neatly stacked papers weighted with polished rocks, a cigarette stub in an ashtray, a bisque pencil mug. He opened the door of the wet cupboard Channing had so proudly shown him; the smell of wet clay, cloth, sprang out; the humidifier clicked off as the damp air from the room took over. Shelves for scales, tools, weighed pieces of clay on a shelf ready for the wheel.

"Nothing here to help much—" Ray looked up from the desk. "No changes on this calendar—Teaparty thing on Tuesday, library and Revere conference Wednesday–Thursday, Greenfield Friday morning through Saturday noon. Guess he planned to be here straight through next week, from Sunday on it's marked BF, no other dates."

Simon opened his slicker, perspiring underneath the airtight yellow skin, glanced at what he could see of a letter resting underneath a polished chunk of quartz. An open shelf of books, mostly reference, was directly behind him. A sentence or two leaped out from the Bayard Foundation's letterhead: "—Mrs. Hayward has been sending resumés—pressing for a decision—keep you in touch. Faithfully, Grace Wilber." BF. Beemeadows Farm? Bayard Foundation?

The gay San Blas pillows on the couch were the only spot of color in the room, and even they picked up and led the eye outdoors to the border of the deck. It had no railing, but was edged instead with fiberglass planters, their gray convenience drowned in bright petunias, lobelias, impatiens, nodding their heads ruefully in the weight of the rain.

Simon started to slide back the glass door, found it open after all; they followed him out onto the deck, stopped. "So that's what happened to your upholstery tacks, Ray." They looked at the felt-textured carpeting, already pocked with rust where the sharp indigo tacks were scattered over the deck like caltrops on a medieval battlefield.

Avoiding the tacks, they moved to the corner of the deck cantilevered out over the old millpond, where two flower boxes were missing. Looking down, they saw them in ruin, the potting soil almost purple in the rocky gloom, the petals of flowers spangling the rain-black granite.

And farther down, almost perpendicular, his head well submerged in the water, Channing Adaams' body lay sprawled, upside down, his body bare except for his old tennis shorts, the waxy skin of the dead whiter even against the dark rocks and brown water but glistening in the drizzle. His arms were flung out as for a dive, his hands and head floating in the water. Even from the deck they could see the bloating of his hands and forearms, the soles of his bare feet punctured with carpet tacks, though the rain had washed away any blood there might have been.

# CHAPTER V

"I'd think, Perce, *if* one's living in community as we are all *trying* to do, even in a crisis like this there'd be some consideration of other people's needs. It's imperative I contact Dr. Blanford, Webby has shut himself up in the silo and Webster and I can't determine whether forcing him will have a productive or counterproductive effect. We'll certainly, all of us, have to have a Colloquium on Death but that can come later. Right now I need to telephone Dr. Blanford."

"Mrs. Hayward." Perce put his hand on the office telephone. "May I say with authority for the whole of Beemeadows that the longer your small spawn remains chewing on his guilt in the silo, the better for us all. If I had the skill to do so I would personally go out there with mortar and trowel and brick him in. Channing is dead, the victim of your son's joke with the carpet tacks, we are trying to find Louisa, there is only one telephone in this house, you are not welcome in my apartment *or* Ada's, and you can easily use the pay phone outside the store in Chetford if you'll stir your rump. Finally, it is my personal opinion that your little Webby would have been much better off left in the trousers of your husband's pajamas." Perce calmly picked up the receiver, ignoring Sally's squeal of fury and the banging screen door as she rushed out, and began dialing yet another nursing home.

Helen, making the bed next door, wished to heaven Simon had heard that. Who'd have thought mild old Perce had it in him? She must remember to tell him. Thank heaven the rain was over; the sun blazed on the lilac tree, wisps of steamy mist were rising from the meadows outside the window.

She picked up their breakfast tray and stumped through the office, past Perce's indefatigable telephone—he'd been at it since ten this morning when they realized Louisa hadn't left a number or an address for them, which was most unlike her. Thelma had recalled that the New York hospital thrift shop she'd run for so many years owed her a favor or two, and had gotten a list of nursing homes to begin with. Feeling futile and useless, and even worse, indecisive, Helen had spent the morning playing solitaire on the veranda; Webster was attempting to be helpful by writing an obituary.

Simon was in the kitchen unloading the dishwasher from last night's scrappy pick-up supper and trying at the same time to stir something that smelled divinely of saffron on the stove. He took the tray from Helen and handed her a large wooden spoon. "Here, peg leg, you stand there and stir and I'll set the table. Almost noon."

Helen recounted to him Perce's brush with Sally as she absent-mindedly stirred the contents of the heavy copper pot, and in spite of himself Simon managed a rather abstracted chuckle.

"It was the carpet tacks, wasn't it, Simon? Webby's revenge for the thrashing?"

"It seems so—the little devil'd been reading *Sailing Alone Around the World*—there's an incident, apocryphal and very likely journalistic juicing up, where Slocum tells how he scattered tacks on the deck of the *Spray* to prevent the Tierra del Fuegan Indians from boarding and massacring him in his sleep."

"Humph. Wonder what he'd been reading when he dug his animal traps. God, what a ghastly thing, though—Webby's Dr. Blanford's got his work cut out for him this time."

The sound of a vacuum cleaner; Thelma had come over to clean up the dried mud the police, Judah, all of them, had tracked into the house for hours yesterday afternoon and night.

"Where's Ray?"

"Stir from the bottom, luv. Up at the Adaamses', manning the phone there. Reporters, friends, so forth. Heroic job."

"Hey there, Simon, I'll do that." Ada bustled in, the soles of her wooden clogs wet from the grass. "We all having lunch together?"

"Very likely. You haven't closed the store, have you?"

"Saturday. Close at noon anyway. How many of us? You, me, Perce, Helen, Thelma, Ray, how about the Haywards?"

"Haven't missed a meal yet, have they? Sally's gone down to use the pay phone in Chetford, and Webster—after he'd finished writing Channing's obituary—went out to the barn to keep watch over the silo in case the child came down after all."

"Father, you sound absolutely bitchy." Ada almost laughed. "Okay, that's ten, with Webby. Little crud."

"I wonder if Perce is saving this cress for anything?" Simon was rummaging through the refrigerator. "It's now or never, already a bit jaded. Thelma brought down some lettuce, we'll have a salad."

"Use it up, there's tons more cress up in the millpond." Ada stopped, a bowl clutched to her bosom, dropped a folded napkin. "Well, it does only grow up there—can't see it'd upset any of us more than we are already and it's a shame to waste it."

"Right you are. Helen, keep stirring from the *bottom*, child. Add some of that broth now, and you can put in those artichoke hearts."

"Risotto? Good idea." Ada sniffed appreciatively.

"Yes, I thought we needed something filling. Perce felt he

should be the one to tell Louisa when he reaches her, but cousins or not, the dear man's fierce about his kitchen so I thought I'd not try anything more elaborate."

"Too bad Louisa didn't leave a number; that's a hell of a job, calling all those places. How's your leg, Helen?"

"Better, Ada, thanks. Sun helps. God, think of Channing lying out there in the rain."

"Don't." Ada set out an assortment of glasses on the buffet between the kitchen and dining room, decanters of wine, a pitcher of water, beer in quarts, plates, a trivet for the risotto. "Funny, now he'll never finish the rest of these bowls, or the ashtrays he was doing for here and for me—Alf and Thelma and I had a hell of a time about smoking between courses. Louisa and Channing didn't at all, and Perce's given it up, and the Scotts only like those little black cigars after dinner, Ray, too, or a pipe—" She added four willow-pattern soup plates to the half dozen Channing had made and glazed deep blue, put salt and pepper on the table. "Well, to hell with being grand today, I'm gonna put the coffee cups at the places now. Dessert or not, Helen?"

"Who, me? It'd take me an hour to make Minute Rice if I tried. Simon's the cook of us, Ada."

"Um . . . no. No dessert. There's a peck of peaches on the back porch if anyone's desperate, and that Vermont cheese. Helen, give over that spoon, I don't trust you."

He stirred his risotto, pouring minuscule amounts of boiling broth in from time to time. The screen door to the back porch slammed; Ray wiped his shoes on the mat and sat down in the armchair. "To hell with it up there, let the phone ring for a while. Mostly ghouls anyway." He rubbed his face tiredly as Simon smashed a large clove of garlic with a rolling pin and tossed it into the salad dressing. "That smells good."

Judah's truck pulled up outside with the clatter of a loose tailgate. He knocked on the back door, stuck his head in.

"Hey there, Ray, everybody." Katey followed him in, looking whiter and more silvery than usual but also a bit diminished, that's what, Helen thought.

"Come on in, fellas, lunch's almost ready." Ada reached for more glasses, plates.

"Well, I got some news might want to get out of the way first. Everybody else gonna be here? Just as soon tell it once only. Sally was right on our tail coming up the drive."

"Sure, let me get Perce, he's been on that phone too long already." Ray picked up his cigar and went out into the hall, giving Thelma, who was putting the vacuum away, a pat on the hip as he went. "Nip out to the barn and haul in Webster, will you, Thel? Judah's here with some news and then we'll have lunch."

"Lord, we all look ghastly," Thelma said without apology as she went through the kitchen and out to the barn. We do, Helen thought. Ada's nice big-boned face and sturdy square figure seemed to support the strain better than anyone else's. There was more life in her black olive eyes than in all the others put together. Even Judah seemed to have misplaced most of his nice, easy aura that was so pleasant and comfortable. Perce, as one would expect, was wound up like a frantic gray wire, casting a fiercely possessive glance at the stove, his kitchen, Simon's chopping something on the counter, all with his mind clearly somewhere else. Ada stopped him at the buffet, handed him a glass of beer without a word, poured one for Judah, for herself. Katey shook her head. Simon took a glass of wine, poured half of it into the pot on the stove, sipped and passed it to Helen.

Sally was babbling to Webster about the therapist's advice as they followed Thelma in. "No, it's all right to leave him there for a bit, Dr. Blanford said, as long as he knows we've just come in for lunch and will be right back with his. Oh, Simon, Webby hates saffron, you'll have to make him a sandwich or something else."

Ray sat down with a sigh. "Sally, shut up. Judah has some news for us and I think Webby's diet can wait until after we've heard what he has to say."

"Well, it's like this." Judah cleared his throat. "You may not have heard, but there was a hell of a bus smash over to Middlefield this morning, two of 'em ran bang into each other and rolled off the road and overturned, and every doctor in Pittsfield's probably at the hospital now. The medical examiner's up to his neck in bodies, your phones were all tied up so he called me figurin' as I was a commissioner I could get up here and tell Mrs. Adaams—she ain't back yet?"

"No, not yet."

"Well—" Judah referred to the back of an envelope he had scribbled on. "It seems Channing died of a broken neck, caused by that fall from the deck, and that was likely caused by his steppin' in bare feet on them carpet tacks, fallin' to his knees—there was tacks there and in his elbows and forearms and hands—and then knockin' over them flower boxes and droppin' from the deck down to the rocks—that's a good twenty feet at least, I'd say. He didn't drown after all, it must have looked like it when you found him, but he broke his neck instantaneously, the doc said. No water in the lungs"—he turned the envelope over, squinting at his own writing—"or froth in the nose and mouth like when you drown."

Sally put a Kleenex to her mouth, gagging.

"Could he tell when it happened?" Ray put out his cigar.

"Figures three days ago, that'd be Tuesday, and probably right after he'd eaten—stomach contents, condition of skin in water, that sort of stuff. He'll send Mrs. Adaams a written report when he gets a minute of course; said to be sure and tell her it was all painless and quick, except them tacks of course. All over in a second, in case anybody's been thinking of him down there alive and nobody knowing. Couldn't a done nothing even if they'd known."

"Cold comfort for Louisa, but better than nothing."

Thelma stood up, smoothed out the front of her skirt. "Katey, aren't you staying, dear?" She addressed herself, though, to a stubbed-out cigarette in the ashtray next to Judah, the sound of the girl's feet running across the grass and the damp gravel of the drive toward her cabin.

"Poor child, first her cat and now this—it *is* rather grim and she's so young. No, Judah, leave her alone." Thelma pressed him back down onto a stool. "I'll go over later, but right now let's have lunch. Simon! I think you're letting that scorch."

*

"Ha! Didn't trust *me* to stir, and *you* burned the risotto!" Helen poked Simon's ribs. "It was good anyway, darling." They had left Ada and Ray to the dishes, Thelma taking over the Adaamses' telephone and Perce the office's, Sally to her bed with a migraine, and Webster with a peanut butter sandwich in the barn "where he looks like he's an old rooster trying to hatch an egg, squatting at the bottom of the ladder clucking up to the top of the silo," Simon had commented as he'd backed their car out of its stall and headed for the main road.

"Why are we going to Pittsfield, anyway, Simon?"

Without answering, he swung the car over the woodsy entrance to a trail leading off the road, stopped, and reached into the back seat and pulled out an old flight bag. "Keep an eye out, will you? This looks remote enough." He opened the door and got out, began to pull off his chino slacks.

"Simon! Here? And now? You impetuous lad!"

"Oh, hush up, Helen." He fastened a pair of black trousers, put a black rabat over his T-shirt, dug the stud into the back of a clerical collar, and pulled on a black jacket. "Oh, damn and blast—" He was holding a pair of black socks, the flight bag was empty, the white sneakers on his feet screamingly out of place.

"Don't panic, just put the socks on over your sneakers, it'll look like you're wearing black suede fruit boots. What are you up to, anyway? I haven't seen you in drag for *weeks!*"

"Clever girl." He wiggled his feet. "They'll do, they'll do. What I need, my dear," he said as he squinted his blue eyes in the rearview mirror and pulled back on the road, "is all the clout I can get. While my party suit may not help, chances are it will. If nothing else, I can always refer to some ancient Hippolytan prayer—of my own invention, of course—that, by canon law, must be intoned over the body of a soul sent home to God by death upon the water. But let's hope it doesn't come to that."

"You want to look at Channing again? I hope you and Ray didn't do anything dreadful carrying him up to the house before the police got there, by the way."

"Yes, I do, and no, I don't think we did at all. Didn't know for certain he was dead—always a chance, although I must say, even from the deck— Well, no harm done, but yes, I do want to look at Channing's body again, and you, my stout-heart, may come with me for succor if you behave yourself."

"Goody gumdrops." Helen felt the pit of her stomach sink away, rallied to his need. "What a necrophilic vacation we're having, aren't we? Outstrips the time I spent a naughty week-end in Washington with someone who shall be nameless; we spent an entire afternoon in the Army and Navy Medical Museum trying to find the two-headed baby in a bottle."

"And did you?"

"No, as a matter of fact. There was an absolutely fascinating skeleton of a Civil War soldier completely ossified by arthritis, for starters. They'd had to pull out two front teeth so he could feed through a straw, couldn't even move his jaw, much less any other joint in his body. And then we went on to the venereal disease exhibit—well, darling, it *was* on the way to the two-headed baby—and by the time we'd done all the chancres and noseless faces in wax replicas and softened skulls and all the museum was closing and we had to leave."

"I see. Next time I feel like giving you a treat, then, we'll go to Washington and continue the tour."

"Thrills." Channing's body twice will be quite sufficient, though, she thought, feeling her intestines in tight knots.

"Feel better?"

Oh, damn him, he knows me through and through and through. She didn't know whether to be grateful for his sensitivity to her or resentful that she had so little privacy of emotions from him.

"Yes—I find silly vulgarity is a splendid solution to some of life's uglies. Thanks." She lit a cigarette, sat in silence as they rode slowly past a rolling field full of hefty Black Angus. "Simon, why *do* you want to see Channing again?"

"Not quite sure, but something isn't right. I wish now we'd stopped at the Adaamses' first, I'd like to have tried something. I find it difficult to envision what we're telling ourselves happened could have happened—that Channing stepped out to the deck, barefoot as was his custom, landed on the tacks directly outside, fell down to his knees and elbows—and then calmly crawled onward toward the edge of the deck, through more tacks, rather than back to the workroom."

"You're right, you know. It's much more likely he'd just sit down and hunker back—I would have, anyway."

"Of course. There's something else, as well. The doorjambs leading out to the deck when we found him yesterday were damp with the air coming in from the door and window, but I was up there with Ray all morning until lunch. They'd dried out in the sun and there were some very impressive handprints on either side, pressed into the oak."

"Handprints? Come on, Simon, you with your little deerstalker and magnifying glass?"

"Handprints—of clay. They wouldn't have shown yesterday; the color of the oak's stain is clay color itself when it's damp, but it was much lighter this morning, like silver birch. The prints look—well, not as if someone were simply touching the wood for a moment before going out, they looked fumbling, ground into the grain of the wood itself. With what I think are a few specks of blood."

"Blood? Had he cut himself? And *had* he been potting? There wasn't anything on the wheel."

"No. But there should have been. When he showed me around so proudly last week he was very pleased with his 'wet cupboard,' as he calls it—clay bin, humidifier, shelves for cloths, scales, and so on. There were six weighed pieces of clay sitting on one of the shelves."

"Weighed?"

"Yes, apparently one does that if one is making a set of identical objects—plates, vases, so forth—helps having them all come out the same size. There were six pieces like birds on a fence, all very tidy."

"And?"

"When I looked yesterday, there were only five. The clay bin itself was empty as well—it was last week; Channing said he was going to bring back some from Newton after the Teaparty conclave, there's a supply house there that stocks a superior variety."

"Hmm. Maybe he—well, gave one to Webby to play with?"

"Unlikely, after going to the trouble of weighing them so exactly. He said he'd given Webby some clay earlier in the summer anyway, the boy keeps it in the cellar of the main house. And even if the lad weren't well supplied, d'you think Channing would offer, or Webby accept, a present after the historic thrashing?"

"Well, no. Channing might, but Webby—he's not that complex yet. Still at the simple stage where one emotion at a time is enough. In his case, mischief and revenge seem to alternate. By the way, remind me to get some adhesive tape in town, you used the last of it on my cast. Okay, so seeing Channing and Louisa leave for the day—I doubt anyone took the trouble to tell him it was supposed to be for the rest of the week—on Tuesday morning, he marched up with Ray's carpet tacks in his little paw, thinking the coast was clear. Why *did* Channing come back Tuesday, anyway? Anybody have any idea?"

"None I've heard. Easy enough to do, of course, just take the back road to Middlefield after dropping Louisa in Lee at the bus stop, and come home by way of the old post road, it runs right past the Adaamses', roughish but still passage, instead of coming in the main entrance to the farm. Perhaps he just wanted a day alone—people often do. Perhaps he'd forgotten some papers—but if it were just that he wouldn't have changed and spent the day."

"What is it? You always chew on your cheek when you're holding back, Simon."

"Do I? There were at least two other people up there Tuesday besides Webby—and neither has said anything about it. Yet. One of them was Perce."

"*Perce?*" He never goes anyplace except between his apartment and the kitchen. What makes you think Perce?"

"Ada. Remember she was a bit late getting back to take over the store on Tuesday, delirious with the mowing machine? She was in fine fettle; explained she'd had to lurk behind a spinney with the machine turned off because Perce was protecting the asparagus patch. Seems to think she doesn't know about it, and I don't doubt he'd have ruptured himself if he'd known she was there."

"What are you talking about?"

"In the small meadow near the spinney there is a large outcrop of granite, around which grows some very fine wild asparagus beloved not only of Perce and the rest, but also of the woodchucks. My cousin, after reading *Territorial Imperative* or some such tome, and after a few experiments, discovered that frequent applications of his bodily fluid established, in the woodchucks' minds, his 'ownership' of the asparagus. Ada says twice a week does it. He drinks up a bottle of ale, and by the time he gets to the near meadow his somewhat senior kidneys have done their work and he's full of the necessary. He mounts the outcrop, untrusses his points, and lets fly. Pity we weren't here while there was still enough asparagus to make a meal—it must be delicious if Perce takes the trouble to protect it all summer."

"Oh, I love it! Perceval Giffard in his old school tie and blazer and gray flannel bags peeing around the asparagus. I do hope it isn't *on* it?"

"No, no, weaves an outer circle round it thrice. Rather charming, I knew you'd love it. Well, in any event, Ada was discreet, consequently a bit late, we had a good laugh about it, and it wasn't until this morning I remembered she'd said he had an empty basket in the other hand and was probably going on up to pick watercress—it was a sizzling morning, he wouldn't have made one trip that far and then done it over again."

"Just because he had a basket?. It could have been for apples, or anything."

"All the apples farther on are wormy and they're far from ripe, and you haven't a scrap of gastronomic memory, have you? Those sandwiches I brought out to the lawn were larded with fresh watercress, there was a huge bag of it in the fridge, and when I got our breakfast that morning there was no watercress at all."

"Okay. He was up at Channing's Tuesday morning. He did make an appointment with somebody on the telephone early that morning, he was in the office and I was on the porch before Louisa brought the car down; he said something about 'eleven o'clock.' But of course that could have been for anywhere, I guess. But if it was some sort of date for back at his house, wouldn't Channing have seen Perce and the other way around? Drat this cast, I can't go tramping around—"

"No, not necessarily—the path down to the pond where the cress grows leads from the stream directly under the deck; all quite hidden from the house and deck unless you're actually looking over the edge."

"But if Channing's body had been there, wouldn't Perce have screamed bloody murder?"

"Of course. Unless it *had* been bloody murder and Perce had pushed him off."

"My God, but why?"

"Why indeed? Nevertheless, the possibility is there. Webby, and I'm sure it'll distress him when he knows he's made things easier rather than harder, *has* owned up to the tack gig—before he barricaded himself into the silo last night I got him alone; he says he saw Channing through the workroom window, it must have been just before noon, and lay in wait in the ferns and rhododendrons until Channing left the room to go to the loo or fix his sandwich or something. Then Webby nipped up, strewed his deadly seeds, and buggered off. There was something I had the feeling he *wasn't* telling me, but that much sounded genuine. Where are we? What glorious hydrangeas—Dalton?"

"Yes, there's the sign. Left turn. You said there was another person who'd been up there. If the medical examiner is right and Channing died after a meal, and the meal was lunch, it'd be someone who smokes, I gather?"

"Clever girl. The cigarette end in the ashtray. Channing and Louisa didn't—and we should try harder to emulate them in that respect, by the way—"

"I know, I know. But let's see—Ada smokes, and Thelma, Ray'd probably have a cigarette if he didn't have a cigar or a pipe, Perce gave it up. But need it have been someone from Beemeadows anyway? Channing could have picked up somebody and brought them back with him, you know. And even so, we still don't have anything but supposition about someone pushing him over the deck, darling."

"A supposition that's extremely uncomfortable, for me, however, until you or someone else explains why and how he got to that corner of the deck, and for what, when freedom from those tacks lay directly behind him. And another thing —Ada and Judah parted company at some point that morning; as I said, she was late getting down to the store, but Judah came roaring back to the garage in a fine temper a bit past noon, beaver down and lance couched, so to speak."

"A spat with Ada? I can't imagine it—they're like two middle-aged puppies together, laughing and scratching and carrying on. Perce did say everyone had had hopes—"

"So I gather. Hard to tell why he was angry, but he was. Enough to put out the 'Closed' sign in front of the garage and shut himself in with a bottle of rye. He was well on the way to being six sheets to the wind by the time I left. When I told Ada I thought perhaps she could go jolly him out of it, she only shrugged and buried her nose in *The Racing Form*."

The outskirts of Pittsfield began to smear the roadside; useful, but so very very ugly. Helen sighed.

"You said two people were up there who didn't say anything about it—you forget there was one who did. Sally. I thought I told you; she went up about five to borrow Channing's foundation directory; when she came back she said the front door had been unlocked but the workroom, where all those books were, was hot as an oven, all closed up."

"Closed?"

"Yep. So who came back and opened the door to the deck after Sally left? Who indeed?"

*

Simon was right. The medical examiner, a quiet, harried man named Connolly, took the clericals seriously and hastily gave Simon a pass for the morgue attendant, as well as a quickly Xeroxed copy of his post-mortem findings. "Very unfortunate, very, a distinguished man, Mr. Adaams, and in splendid physical condition. You'll have to excuse me, Father Bede; I was just in the middle of his autopsy when they started bringing in the bodies from the bus collision; I'm needed at the hospital now more than here, one of the anesthesiologists is on vacation for one thing—let me know later if there's anything more—" He virtually burst away from them toward the exit, leaving his stained white coat on the hall floor and pulling on a jacket as he went.

*

How extraordinary, Helen thought, that the last worldly privilege Channing Adaams would ever claim would be his very own slab in a corner of the Pittsfield morgue. The room was a havoc of the remnants of the bus collision; bodies were being doubled up on stretchers, tables; children with adults, and where the morgue attendant had run out of cover sheets, Helen thought how hard it would be to find any relationship except that all were joined in death.

Only Channing seemed to have retained his identity, in spite of the Y-shaped incision from the shoulders to the breastbone and down the abdomen, the "baseball stitch" sewing it up neatly if not aesthetically. Channing, and yet he looked as the dead do. He looked taken out of context, she found herself thinking, the way a familiar piece of furniture one is accustomed to seeing in a well-known room looks when one comes across it sitting on the sidewalk waiting for a moving van. Unreal, the same and yet not the same. His hair had dried to its old gold of many colors, but it meant nothing.

Simon was holding one of Channing's hands, as if reading his palm. He laid it down, picked up the other. Helen moved closer; this must be why he wanted her with him. She saw the skin peeling away from the long immersion in the water, yet leaving the puncture marks from the tacks and a multitude of short splintered cuts quite visible, the flesh around them standing proud.

"Do you see these, Helen? Splinters—a bit bigger than toothpick tips; I noticed them yesterday when we thought he might have drowned. It's quite true that drowning people actually *do* clutch at straws, you know. One almost always finds weed, grass, in their death grip, and quite often cuts from such tight seizure of even a water lily pad."

"But he didn't drown, he was dead before his head touched the water."

"Yes. And the splinters are only in his hands. They're wood, and there was no wood around—the doorjambs are intact, the flower boxes are fiberglass, the deck is entirely carpeted, and there was nothing below where he fell but rocks. No wood at all."

# CHAPTER VI

"Simon, does it seem to you as if everything's happening twice?" Thelma automatically flattened a turned-over edge of the Kairouan carpet in front of their fireplace and sat down on the old velvet sofa from Seventy-second Street that Ray had insisted on bringing up, along with his huge rump-sprung easy chair and footstool. "Oh, thank heavens, Ray, I thought you'd gone to sleep in the kitchen." She took a drink from the tray he passed, lit a cigarette.

"Nope, just the ice-bucket handle. Came off, had to fix it. Here you are, Simon. I'll take this out to Helen." They had gone to the little church in Otis that Perce had told Helen of, twenty miles away, the Russells wanting to show Simon the early eighteenth-century building that had never been modernized, electrified, or heated with anything other than the parishioners' own hot bricks, foot warmers, and bodily calories. The child assigned to pump air for the little organ in the loft was probably the only warm one in the congregation. Closed as it was now, except for summer Sundays when a supply priest was traded a holiday in the tiny rectory in return for eight Sunday services, it held the chill of two hundred years of Berkshire winters, springs, and falls. In spite of the sun blazing on its roof this morning, Helen had come out with a violent set of shivers and was perched on the Russells' front steps, trying to get the cold out of her bones. Simon had loved the austerity of it, the white walls, bubble-flawed clear glass windows, agonizing pews. He had had to agree with Helen that it was just as well it wasn't a sung mass; the young priest had yet to overcome a voice that sounded like tapioca put through a blender.

"I certainly do, Thelma. It's like a glass reflecting a glass reflecting a glass—first Channing disappears, but we don't know it for days; now Louisa's turned out to have done the same thing."

"Dear God, I hope not with the same ending. But that's what's on our minds now. Perce looks simply dreadful, worse every day."

"What I can't understand about Louisa," Ray sank into his woolen womb of a chair and put his feet up, "is that Channing's death has been in the papers since Saturday morning, yesterday, and I heard it myself on the radio before we left for church this morning. She can't have missed seeing or hearing it; even if she did someone would tell her."

"I don't know quite what we're going to do if she doesn't come back soon—about the funeral, for one thing. I don't think Channing wanted to be cremated, but it's not really for any of us to say or cope with without Louisa's say-so. Webster, of course, wants to start the police looking for her— Ray and Perce have been against it up until now, she'd hate all that publicity, but really, Perce has combed every possible connection he can think of, far beyond nursing homes too. He doesn't look like a gray terrier for nothing." Thelma put down her drink, stirring the molasses-colored Bourbon unseeingly with a sprig of fresh mint.

"Helen, are you warm enough to come in? I'll light the fire—" Ray called out the open front door.

"No, thanks, Ray, I'm fine now. What's up?" She sat down next to Simon on the sofa.

"Thel and I want to chew something over, and you two seem to have hard heads and a fresh eye for all this. I went into Lee yesterday afternoon; new set of drill bits I'd ordered had been dropped off at the bus stop and I hadn't thought to ask you to pick them up for me on your way back from

Pittsfield. Well, the bus stop is also the drugstore, right on the main drag, and of course the lady that runs it was all agog over Channing and so on; we've all been in and out for years with our prescriptions and one thing and another, she knows us all. Wasn't being nosy or morbid, but did ask about Louisa and how she was, and I said that she'd gone down to New York on Tuesday and she wasn't back yet but that I'd pass on her condolences. Well, that seemed to set her back a bit. 'New York?' she said. 'She went to Albany, same as usual on Tuesday, sold her a ticket myself and saw her get on the Albany bus, the driver had to give her a hand, her knees were bad. I was out seeing about some packages. . . . Mr. Adaams dropped her off in front of the store and buzzed on like a bat out of hell. Louisa usually got here earlier and had a cup of coffee but she was late on Tuesday and both the buses, express to New York and the Albany bus, pulled up just as she got here.' The lady's certain it was Albany."

"*Albany?* Lord, it is like a multiple looking glass. D'you imagine she wanted some time to herself as perhaps Channing did, and is holed up in a hotel in Albany? Would your friend Colonel Bemis know?" Simon rubbed his head.

"That's what bothers Ray, Simon." Thelma brooded over her drink. "Neither Ray nor I can imagine any possible need Louisa would have to go to Albany; so far as we know, and we've known her for years, I truly don't think she knows a soul there. After all, who does, in Albany? Except Alf, but Ray called him yesterday and asked if he'd seen Louisa, but Alf said no, he hadn't heard a word from her. And to press any further—"

"What's gotten at my wife is the biggest hogwash I've ever heard. Sally started making some cracks before dinner last night before you two got back from Pittsfield; the burden of them was that possibly the reason Louisa wasn't findable was that she was having an affair with someone somewhere—"

"Which *is* the *biggest* piece of hogwash I've ever heard,

but it got to me, you know. If by the wildest possibility Louisa and Alf are in Albany together, at least Alf would have the decency to tell her about Channing and she'd be back by now. But I don't believe it."

"Aw, no question," Ray snorted. "Straight as a die, Louisa. Sally's just seeing how far she can get a needle in us, especially Perce. He almost brained her with a griddle when she brought it up."

"I confess that possibility was on our minds; glad you could bring it out into the air. As you say, from the little I saw of Louisa it does seem extraordinarily unlikely. But I gather that her leaving without any note of her whereabouts is even more unlikely." Simon put down his glass, shook his head at Ray's offer of a second drink.

"Yes, it is." Thelma passed a dish of nuts across the coffee table. "All the years Ray was Channing's investment adviser more than half the time Channing would be off in some inaccessible place when Ray had to have a quick yes or no to trade something on the market, but Louisa was *always* reachable, always."

"Well," Helen nibbled on a nut, "from what I saw of her before she left, I can sure believe she *might* like a vacation from everything, and if it weren't for her trouble driving it'd be perfectly possible she went over to Albany, rented a car, and is just driving around the boondocks to get away from it all—good time for it, Channing was going to be away himself, and if she were up in Vermont, for instance, she wouldn't necessarily have heard. Those local sheets wouldn't put it on the front page, Channing wasn't the damn President, after all, and how often do you run across a big metropolitan daily in a general store in Function Junction, anyway? Even Ada keeps her copies of the *Times* under the counter for the regular customers."

"I know, but we get right back to it, that she couldn't drive very far or much this summer—" Thelma took a nut, mentally counted its calories, and put it back in the dish.

"As long as we're letting our hair down, I guess I'd better reveal my lack of surprise that she isn't down in New York or Long Island putting her old nanny out to pasture. It's embarrassing, but some of the finer points of etiquette rubbed off me somewhere along the line. Friday morning I was staying in bed; there wasn't anything handy to read and Simon was sporting his oak up in the silo—well, right next to our bed there's a filing cabinet. I read a lot of the letters that are in it—I also look in people's medicine chests." She grinned, both ruefully and defiantly, at Simon.

"Oh, heavens, Helen"—Thelma laughed—"so do I, and probably most people. No harm in any of that, unless one gossips about the findings, and when you come right down to it, I think men are much worse than women about tattling."

"Agreed!" Ray thumped up the pillow behind his back. "Water cooler or men's room in any business office would put any girls' bridge club to shame."

"Thanks. Anyway, the thing is this. There was, among the letters, a note to Louisa from her old nanny's nephew, thanking her for the wreath for the funeral and enclosing some pictures of Louisa as a baby that Nanny had had before she died. It was dated four years ago."

"Whew! Four years ago?" Ray sat up.

"Yep. I remember thinking to myself at the time that Louisa'd probably had more than one nanny; the snapshots just showed one of those capped and caped dames with a bundle of expensive laundry in her arms, near enough to a newly born Louisa so there'd be room for other nursemaids in her young life—her father moved around so much and maybe this one didn't like to travel, or only took care of infants. But then Perce—well, he's been asking all those nursing homes for Miss Pearl Rourke, and that was the name of the old lady that died four years ago. And given Perce's profession, it doesn't seem likely he'd have the name wrong, would he?"

"Not Perce. No, he'd have dredged up the right name from somewhere in his head, no matter how long ago he'd heard it." Ray twisted uneasily in his chair. "He may be kind of withdrawing and diffident if he's presented with the actual person in the flesh, but names themselves are as unforgettable to him as stock market listings used to be to me."

"That's what I thought." Helen lifted her cast and put it on a magazine on the coffee table, leaned back. "So what I'm wondering is, did Channing know Pearl Rourke was dead or not? And if so, does that mean they were up to something together, he and Louisa? Something that needed this sort of excuse so Louisa could be somewhere else without anybody noticing anything?"

"Well, off the top of my head, I'd say Channing didn't know." Ray sucked on an ice cube for a moment, thinking. "If it was four years ago the lady died, and she wasn't a part of Channing's past, only Louisa's, it's exactly the sort of background detail he'd forget even *before* Louisa told him, if she bothered him with it at all. But the reason I think he didn't know was that on his engagement calendar up at their house —Simon and I went through it like Holmes and Watson yesterday morning while we were manning the phone there— Channing had noted down the times Louisa went to New York—or told him she did—the last two or three months, and they always said, 'Louisa/Nanny, NY'—why would he do that in a very private date book? Louisa kept the public one for the whole community down in the office at the main house; I doubt anybody got a look at the one on Channing's desk except him and Louisa. And he did seem to resent her going when he referred to it in public—always wanted her full attention and time, Channing did."

"What doctor did she go to, by the way?" Helen asked.

"Pulaski, in New York—I remember because I got her pre-

scriptions refilled a couple of times for her in Lee and his
name was on the labels—reminded me of the horrible Pulaski
Skyway."

Simon stood up. "So whatever it is that's keeping her away
must be infinitely more important to Louisa than Channing's
priorities right now." He helped Helen to her feet. "And
given their past life, that's pretty important, I'd venture."

*

"Look, I'm sorry, but I just can't hack it here." Katey's little car was pulled up by the back porch, and Perce and Ada
stood beside it, Perce holding a bag of groceries Katey had
handed him and Ada fingering the keys to Bemis's cabin.
"I've got a girl friend in Great Bedford, she works at the
Griffon too, and I can crash with her for a couple of days till I
find something over there. I called the Colonel and he said it
was okay to leave, he understood and I can split the rest of
the rent with him, it's only a month anyway. So that's the
stuff from the fridge and anything else I forgot I guess I don't
want." The back seat, Helen saw, was piled with a stereo,
duffel bags, and what she always thought of as Irish luggage,
shopping bags with blue jeans and underwear spilling out.

"Katey, are you sure?" Ada eyed the girl's white, drawn
face doubtfully. "You've always been mighty welcome here,
you know."

Katey looked back, suddenly aware of someone other than
herself. "Thanks, Ada, I always wondered about that with
you. No, I'm sure. First my cat dies, and now Mr. Adaams,
and besides, there's a guy at the Griffon I've got my eye on;
maybe I'll make out better if I'm over there instead of out in
the toolies here." Ada, disbelieving, finally pocketed the keys.
"And if either of you see Judah would you tell him the garbage cans over there are full, I threw away a lot of stuff."

"Won't you stop at the garage and say good-bye?"

"Rather not, Ada. And tell Mrs. Adaams when she gets back, would you, I'm real sorry. About Mr. Adaams."

Ada and Helen watched the little car scoot down the drive and, turning sharply onto the county road, disappear. "Too bad she couldn't have told Judah herself," Ada said. "He'll go on a six-day bender, I'll bet."

"Maybe not. Too bad, but I can see how the general gloom around here would get to a kid like that—Simon said she couldn't even touch her own cat when it died."

"I used to be squeamish too, before life got to me—nursing Ma got rid of that in a hurry, I can tell you. Well, it was nice of her to do what she could about the rent with Alf; I'll try to get over to the cabin and see if she closed all the windows and the damper. That fireplace has a terrible downdraft in a storm, and the sky's getting all broody again."

And, Helen thought, if you're smart you'll wait till you hear Judah coming up in the truck for his usual afternoon visit, Sunday or not, before you do go over. Nothing like a nice shoulder to cry on to give you a second chance, and him, the big cluck.

*

"No, no, it's no mystery, just half olive oil and half butter instead of all butter. You can bring the temperature up just that extra few degrees without it burning the butter that makes all the difference—now a classic Wiener schnitzel needs pure lard, of course, but that's entirely different. Veal piccate, francese, all those variations of scaloppine—half butter, half oil. You'll see."

Perce and Simon had put together a surprisingly festive late lunch for the four of them from Perce's refrigerator, including four pieces of unexpectedly good veal Katey had left in the grocery bag. "Must have pinched them from the kitchen at the Griffon," Perce had chuckled, "no veal around here in any of the markets." Ray and Thelma had taken a picnic and gone over to Tanglewood for the afternoon, the Haywards had left after breakfast for New York and Dr. Blanford first thing Monday morning. Perce had given Sally a list of locally unobtainable delicacies for her to bring back from the city tomorrow night, but had scant hope she'd remember, particularly since he hadn't included any cash. "I must get after Thelma," he told Simon. "Ray's made no secret about her Christmas present this year being a small greenhouse and she can find a corner for a few things for the kitchen—fresh ginger, for instance, and basil—"

Perce threw open the door of his apartment and followed Simon in. Summer vanished, absorbed and digested by the walls lined with leather-bound books from floor to ceiling, grudgingly making way for a fireplace, two windows, a narrow door. Perce disappeared behind a floor-to-ceiling free-standing bookcase, Simon heard a rattle of crockery, running water, a click of a cupboard door. He peered into a small, monkish bedroom with its single bed covered severely in white cotton twill; a pair of handsome military brushes on a walnut campaign chest bore the Giffard arms.

Perce reappeared with two bottles of opened Guinness, already beading sweat, and two heavy stoneware mugs, waved Simon into the single armchair, covered in worn, mole-colored wide-wale corduroy. He sat himself on the only other place possible, on a tall clerk's stool behind the vast library table that took up virtually all the rest of the living room, its massive shadow drowning out a rather good Persian carpet on the floor. An ancient Underwood stood at attention on a government-surplus typewriter table; behind the clerk's stool khaki file cabinets with neat labels barricaded Perce in to the waist.

"Your mother, I take it?" Simon examined a triptych of ladies framed on the low mantelpiece. Louisa, of course, with Adaams Park in the background, looking a bit more like an attenuated Queen Elizabeth than usual. A turn-of-the-century young matron with baby Perceval on her lap, doubt in her tentative young eyes about what exactly to do with his head. And a young, dark beauty in a white veil that could have been for confirmation, she was so young, except for the bridal wreath of orange blossoms, the wedding bouquet.

"Yes, that's mother." Perce was clearly not going to introduce the third photograph; he poured his stout, put a paperweight on a folder.

"Helen will hear the telephone should it ring? . . . Good. Now, as far as Albany, no. It's one of those places nobody knows well unless they must, dreadful place. Certainly not a fleshpot of earthly delights, not that Louisa is one for hairdressers or shopping and all that. Of course I called Bemis, long before Ray told you about the bus to Albany. He's devoted to Channing and Louisa. But the poor man's locked in twenty-four hours a day with his father, not likely to run into her haphazardly. Cancer; the old man refuses to have a doctor—Christian Scientist—and unfortunately for Alf, without a doctor's verified diagnosis no help, financial or nursing or social, is available from any of those benevolent helping and caring organizations. Their forms must be filled out at any cost. Thus Alf has the whole job. Frightful. He can just afford a practical nurse during the middle of the day, but not for more than a few weeks longer. We all wanted him to bring his father here, where we could all help in shifts around the clock, put him in your room in the main house, but old Mr. Bemis insists on ignoring the entire thing and refuses to budge. Alf has whittled two chess sets this summer. Hopes to sell them."

"Sounds a stout man, not to push his father into a hospital in spite of his wishes."

"Indeed. Yet, if nothing else, it's reinforced our content with Beemeadows. Ray, for instance, swears he can trust us not to turn him into an eggplant in a wheelchair if he chops a leg off cutting firewood, for instance, and Thelma vows she's going to have a nice, polite stroke in the spinach patch and would we please leave her lay where Jesus flang her, to quote Ada. And I assure you when I feel the grim reaper stalking, I intend to go down cellar and put my head in the kiln and turn on the gas."

"Ha! Refuse to clutter up your precious Garland in the kitchen, hmm?"

"Quite." Perce gave one of his quiet, dry smiles, mostly at himself.

"And Channing?"

"Difficult. I don't think Channing had come to the point where he knew he was mortal. Oh, he believed it, of course, but didn't *know* it. Not surprising, full of health and no illnesses to draw him up short for that moment of revelation. Led an extremely centrifugal life, right to the end."

"And I take it Louisa was the still point? Holding it together? Can she be doing any research, for instance, in Albany for Channing?"

"Certainly not. She'd have used the Park, did plenty of times for him over the years, papers, lectures, all that. Nothing in Channing's line we don't have better of—" His voice trailed away, the unspoken "back at home" ringing loud in the silence. "Or Greenfield," he continued, gathering his voice together. "But Channing found quite enough eager students over there to do any small odd jobs for him. Actually, Greenfield was quite enthusiastic last year about having Louisa hold a class or two for them—advanced Portuguese and Spanish literature. She's quite good, you know, but Channing wouldn't have it. Too much of a load for her on top of running the show here. I think she'd have liked it, though."

\*

It makes sense. Helen closed all but one of the albums that covered the quilted bed and stacked them neatly on Simon's pillow. He must have come in from Perce's without her noticing; she could hear him ruminating on the piano in the living room. Bach always made her feel she was inside a tin can in a hailstorm; she lay back on the bed instead of joining him. He'd begun playing after dinner quite a bit, finding the partitas a polite way to quiet all three Haywards before bedtime. Sally never thought; she determined, perceived, surmised, conceptuated, ideated. And so on, interminably. Webster was in some ways more bearable; his overtly prurient interest in a widowed English priest traveling openly with a single lady was at least humanly smutty, although his curiosity had been a bit too much even for Simon's tact at one point. Webster had asked outright if Simon, who as a priest of the Church of England was vowed to say his daily offices without fail in or out of ecclesiastical employment, observed those obligations before or after fornication.

"During, my dear chap, during. Kill two birds with one stone that way," Simon managed with a straight face.

Oddly enough, the only time of day little Webby seemed all of a piece and even possible to have about was when Simon was playing. The boy would take a pillow and, hugging it to him, would sit under the piano itself, the vibrations of the strings and the weaving intricacies of Bach holding him hard, as close to happy as anyone had seen him.

The house was wonderfully peaceful this afternoon, with the Haywards away and no typewriter clicking upstairs. Helen had gone upstairs for the first time with Ada after lunch; the toilet in the upstairs bathroom was running and while Ada jiggled with the innards of it Helen read the title of Sally's book, or a list of possible titles, tacked on the wall over the typewriter.

"Beyond Theory Y: A New Model for Organizational
Development. A Case-Book Approach to
Changing Corporate, Institutional, and Government
Structures."

Helen thought it'd look great in German.

The heavy, airless afternoon pointed up the dead flies on the floors and window sills, the unmade beds and grubby bath and kitchenette of the Haywards' occupancy. *Alors, chacun à son* goo, she thought, returning to her post within earshot of the office telephone.

It did make sense. Now that she'd spent an hour at it and given it her full attention. The yellowed folder of negatives and prints Louisa had stuffed so hastily into the basket arm of the rocker, and that Helen hadn't been able to decide whether to put in the albums and had left on the window sill —light-years ago it seemed—was now spread out on the cool quilt in chronological order, the prints matching their negatives. The first four were unmistakably Central America. Louisa in an early fifties silk suit that had to have come from The Tailored Woman, or Best's, or Abercrombie & Fitch, open-toed shoes, hat, gloves, palm trees in the background. Louisa on the steps of the "residence" with a white-uniformed, grinning staff squinting into the sun. Louisa in a cool, bare tropical drawing room, shaking hands with a plump, uniformed, be-medaled and sashed Latin. Louisa at an airport—the silk traveling suit again—a treacherous-looking airplane—waving, an umbrella held gaily aloft.

Then three of what Helen always thought of as Yalta Bookend shots, the famous front terrace at Adaams Park dressed with United Nations biggies, each backed with their equivalent of an A.D.C., then ranks of spear carriers, Sally among them, barely visible in the back row, very young and with another ill-advised hairdo. Channing was directly behind Eleanor Roosevelt; it had been his previous work with her on the Human Rights Commission that had recalled him briefly to this historic 1951 Conference on Defining Aggression, held in April and August of that year at Adaams Park.

The last nine prints were of Louisa again, in a native village, on a donkey in the mountains, no matter what, always looking as if she were a duchess about to open a bazaar. The final shot was Louisa as well, again waving good-bye, this time from the door of a dreary official building with a Colombian flag hanging listlessly from the roof. Channing had failed to take into account the fierce glare from the corrugated tin roof; half the photograph was overexposed. The presence of a car taking him to the airport was clearly felt; the left side of the picture was out of focus, had an official carrying a suitcase striding hurriedly toward the camera.

The open scrapbook Helen had left in front of her held stories from the New York *Times* about the conference at the Park. Channing's own pictures of it, which might have been taken by Perce since Channing was in them himself, must have been taken at the second and last conference; Mrs. Roosevelt had not been able to be present at the first one in April, and besides, the foliage around the terrace was in full summer lushness. The three prints of the notables and their retinues—Helen recognized a couple of lawyers whose names she couldn't recall, and there was Chip Bollen, Livingston Merchant—but after those three prints and their negatives was a negative without a print.

She picked the strip of film up one more time; ⌗5, ⌗6, and ⌗7 had been the Park, this was ⌗8, and ⌗9 was Louisa in the native village. ⌗8. Helen read the negative with ease. A girl, smiling at the camera, dark and glistening, a flowered dress unexpectedly décolleté for Adaams Park but unmistakably there, the famous involuted gingerbread of the widow's walk providing a perch on the rail for the girl, a bottle of scotch, her mocking cheesecake pose with her skirt well rucked up around sumptuous thighs. Helen looked closer; Thelma was right, it was more likely that the girl had been a bit pregnant than that the style of her dress would add that bit of bulk. The new flowered dress she'd worn at the last day of the conference, Sally had said, when she'd been so tipsy as everyone was leaving after lunch. Around her neck was a string of carved wooden beads and shells, very like some of the work on the masks Simon had hung for Louisa.

It was a flash picture, taken at night; the negative held no secrets from Helen. She looked again at the clippings and pictures from the *Times, Newsweek, Globe,* of the conference making their report the next morning to the Sixth, or legal, Committee of the General Assembly. All precedent had been set aside; they had met in the Security Council room itself, there was Trygve Lie smiling at Mrs. Roosevelt, Channing leaning forward behind her and whispering some pleasantry to bring the famous smile to that great woman's face. Hellmer, Helen's old colleague or rival, she'd never been sure which, had taken that one. Good, too.

Flipping on, the story of Terry's death the night before filled the next page of the album. A very discreet obit from the local paper, "tragic death by accident of Mrs. Perceval G. E. Adaams Giffard, age 22, at Adaams Park during the night. Survived by her husband, Mr. Giffard, and her parents, Mr. and Mrs. Vasco da Cuñha of Madeira, Portugal. Private funeral, no flowers."

So Channing *had* been there in August the night Terry died by falling from the widow's walk. She hadn't been found until early morning, Sally had said, by which time Channing was energetically and aggressively at work defining aggression in the Security Council room in New York, before flying back to Central America and Louisa.

He had been at the April conference, Louisa had saved clippings from the weeklies that mentioned his being there. And if what Sally had said on the lawn—and it was the sort of thing any woman would remember but only a bitch like Sally would repeat twenty-five years or more later—were true about Perce, Channing was very likely the father of Terry's baby.

Poor Terry, besotted with the Adaams glamour, no doubt, growing up there at the Park over a garage or in a servant's room; Perceval must have seemed to a convent-bred eighteen-year-old like a knight in shining armor, and she to him . . . ? Helen looked at the bridal picture. Who could have resisted that soft curve of cheek, the melting eyes of a virginal Madonna. Not Perce. Nor Channing, when he came along. Terry must have settled, for the moment, for a sexless marriage but not a sexless life, and Channing to her by the time she was barely twenty-two would have been exactly what she thought she was getting at eighteen when she set her cap for Perce.

Had she told Channing about the baby that night? Probably. Had he shrugged, disclaimed, left her up there, the fizz gone out of the night, the fun from what was only, after all, a free slap and tickle for him? Helen could imagine his sudden total, icy boredom, the rendezvous so easily and casually made and so quickly broken off, leaving Terry with the scotch and a crying jag, hearing Channing start his engine in some discreet parking place and driving discreetly away.

As he had intended to drive away to Boston after his mid-day tryst with Katey the day he died? "Nice of him to find a sublet for Alf Bemis" Thelma had said. Probably nothing more on his mind than having a "possibility" around the place for the summer. Promising, but not necessary. It would have to work out with discretion, of course, but all that could be managed. Had they used the Scotts' empty house? Very likely. Katey's cabin was out in plain view, but the Scotts were buried in privacy. Yes, there was something very like the Bougereaux satyr about Channing—not just that air of entitlement, but a certain lie-back passiveness, letting it come to him easily without much effort.

Oh he'd make an effort toward discretion, of course; telephoning the girl from the main house Tuesday morning to set an hour for them to meet—eleven, he'd said on the phone—using the office telephone while Louisa was still up at their house, taking no chances along that line.

Helen remembered now what she had thought was white dust fluffing from the hem of Katey's skirt as she got up from the quilt on the lawn, the smell of wild onion. Not dust, dried clay from Channing's workroom, of course, and the smell from a salami sandwich, the white rose spray from Louisa's bushes.

Judah, leaving Ada to her own devices with the mowing machine, must have seen her going up the hillside, followed her long enough for him suddenly to realize his role as red herring—no wonder he roared back to the garage and got drunk.

And, before Katey in her green and gold languor had come to sit beside Helen on the lawn for a moment, she certainly hadn't been contemplating life and death by Magnificat's little grave—Katey had said herself she couldn't take sun on that porcelain skin and there hadn't been even a faint flush on her arms and back and neck. Magnificat's grave by the stump of the dead elm was in full blazing sun all day long.

She had been with Channing as Helen slept on the lawn; Webby, peering through the foliage around the deck, had seen them too, watched them through the glass-walled workroom, seen them disappear to the bedroom, and had seized the moment to strew his tacks about. Finding Helen asleep when he came down, he had used up the rest of his malice toward the world by scrawling "C screws C" on her cast. Channing screws Catey.

Kids nowadays never could spell.

*

The long, brooding afternoon drew down around Beemeadows, stifling, sultry. Even the sweeping meadows seemed depressed, the baling machine was due tomorrow but at the moment the shorn hay lay flat, tired, the life gone from it where it once had been upright and vital. Nor did it seem to hold the promise of nourishment and growth for life in the winter to come. Like Channing, it seemed simply—dead.

Lightning crackled in the distance; chickens pecked listlessly by the barn, going through the motions but with little conviction. Ada, thumbing through *Sports Illustrated*, sat under the hood of her hair dryer, centuries of patience bred into her bones, making it possible to wait until tomorrow. Judah never came up to the farm this late in the day. Now that Katey had gone, the big lunk might come to his senses. Might.

*

Perce, after a jaunt to the asparagus patch, carefully hung up his seersucker jacket, treed his shoes, and with loosened braces lay down on his narrow white bed. In weather like this he *should* have a dehumidifier. Expensive, the quiet ones, though. Better wait and see which way the Muirs jumped. Louisa. . . . wait and see—wait and see—Perce slept.

*

Simon, having put the scrapbooks back on top of the old highboy for Helen, left her chewing her cud and staring at the ceiling after a last remark to him. "Louisa took the print of that negative of Terry, you know, she crumpled it up and shoved it in the pocket of her smock before she stuffed the folder into the arm of the chair. It must have been the necklace that gave away the date to her—there's a snotty letter from old Marguerite in the file cabinet about one just like it Louisa must have sent up with Channing—bitching about how it's amusing but doesn't quite match her emeralds, or something, just as she certainly doesn't match that dreadful Terry and next time couldn't they find her something unique? What a horror she must have been."

\*

Simon took one of Ray's shovels down from the tool rack in the barn and, after opening the trunk of their car and lining it with newspaper, walked across the back meadow to the stump of the old elm.

Someone had been there. At the head of the little cairn of stones Ray had piled over the cat's grave, there was a small crude cross on one side and a Star of David on the other, made of branches tied together with string, flanked by an old peanut butter jar from which drooped a bouquet of tired wild flowers. And a flat stone from the cairn had been tilted up; Simon stooped down to read the crayoned scrawl.

Magnifekat
Rest in Pece
Webby

When Simon was finished, he replaced the offerings as exactly as possible, stood back, and looked sadly at the screaming loneliness they expressed. No, the child need never know *this* specific. It all looked exactly the same.

# CHAPTER VII

"Channing sure as hell was right about one thing," Helen gasped, lowering herself gratefully into an oak armchair in the bar and grill room of the Black Griffon. "I never *would* have made the stairs here the first week." The old inn was something of a core sample of Berkshire architectural history, being added onto, rooms torn off, enlarged, and all opening into each other either up or down a considerable amount of steps.

"Of course not." Simon fairly snapped at her, pulling out a chair for himself. "But if we hadn't stopped for tea with Perceval in the first place you'd never have broken your foot and we could have enjoyed this place—quite charming."

Honestly, Helen thought, he's impossible tonight. As if I'd stepped in that damn hole on purpose. Maybe it's the weather, sultry and oppressive, standing on one foot waiting to drop the other shoe. Well, I'm glad he's enjoying the place itself if not me—we've both been cooped up with Beemeadows' problems too much, this was a good idea. He'd come in from mooching around the barn and made her put on her dress, suggesting they relieve Perce of the worry of feeding them—the Russells would be late getting back from Tanglewood and have supper on their way home, Ada was on a carrot and celery crash diet, and Perce looked wrung out, obviously wanting two poached eggs, a glass of wine, and early bed. Most of all, Simon thought, Perce would like some solitude; he was accustomed to it and hadn't had much at all the last few days.

Helen had forewarned him on the drive over that what he'd get to eat would be a choice of roast beef or fried chicken, baked potato in aluminum foil or hashed browns, creamed corn or stewed-to-a-green-rag zucchini, and a bottle of Virginia Dare. She'd not been able to suppress a laugh of glee when he saw the menu in the wide, quiet dining room with starched linen cloths on the tables, wide-planked old waxed floors, and genuine beamed ceiling. They'd had an unbelievably velvety sorrel soup, parsleyed rack of pink lamb, perfect braised endive, and a raspberry soufflé, with two bottles of Corton Charlemagne.

"You didn't really think I'd have planned on steering us here for the first night of our vacation if I didn't know you'd get a good feed, did you?" she'd teased him as she clumped slowly up and down the slippery old steps toward the bar for coffee. "Don't expect too many places like this, though, if we ever get away from Beemeadows—you'll see more frozen rock lobster tails and canned tomato soup than you'll think possible." She'd felt his arm tighten under her hand; dammit, she never should have said anything about getting away from Beemeadows, he probably thought she hated it, and was feeling guilty. But his face had that dark Welsh look on it now; she'd seen it often enough to know it was useless to do anything but chatter, if that.

"Spot of brandy?" He looked about the dark paneled barroom with its huge fireplace that had warmed generations of skiers over the years and now yawned black. A harpist, of all things, was playing quietly in a corner, two or three tables had people at them, there seemed to be a shortage of waitresses. Sunday night; perhaps one helped oneself from the bar.

"No, I want something foolish, like a pousse-café, or crème de menthe—you know, a real chorus-girl drink. I know! A brandy alexander, with a lot of whipped cream on top, that's what I want. . . . Hi there, Katey. That veal you left at the farm was so good Simon and I came over to try the lamb for dinner." The girl, who had come up behind them with her waitress's pad and long calico dress, looked startled; she hadn't recognized them from behind.

"Oh, hi. Two alexanders?" She looked at Simon, who had stood up to go to the bar himself.

"Lord no, one for Helen and I'll have a Martell. Won't you join us?" He pulled out a chair for her. "Come along, do, it's not busy."

"Well—" She drifted to the bar, twisting her long hair in her fingers as she waited for the drinks, leaning with one elbow on the bar.

"Thyroid," Helen said, lighting a cigarette.

"What?"

"The kid needs thyroid pills or something. I've never seen her with any energy, or a smile. Not that there's been much to smile about when I have seen her—" Dammit, there she went again. "Maybe I'm wrong, with that hair it's probably just being tired. What with a night job and Judah and Channing during the day, I'd be knocked out too."

Well, at least that got a glimmer of a smile from him, she thought, taking her drink from Katey and wishing now she'd ordered an Irish coffee, as Katey had, instead of an alexander. They always gave her a headache.

"Did you get yourself moved in with your friend? That was quite a carload of stuff you had."

"Just partly. I don't know, I may shove on and go out West until school starts again—Chan—Mr. Adaams said those friends from the farm, the Scotts, are on a dig out there and can always use helpers; I took a lot of anthropology before I switched to chemistry. Sounds like it might be more interesting than around here—"

"Your parents are away, I think someone said?" Simon swirled his brandy aimlessly, put the glass down on the table.

"Yeah—they're World Health doctors, in Pakistan. Rented our apartment in New York for the year; they wanted me to go over there and be with them this summer, but it seemed like a lot of trouble for just three months. I don't know."

She's such a child, Helen thought, noticing the bitten fingernails and the tiny mustache of white the cream from the Irish coffee left on her upper lip. Looks like a kitten.

"Simon, you'll hate me but I left my lighter on the table in the dining room—would you?" She kicked him under the table as he glared at Helen's battered old Zippo lying on the table by his package of cigarettes. "Thanks." He got up, strolled out of the room.

"Anthropology and chemistry—that's an interesting combination. What made you switch your major? Anything particular?"

"I guess I just got bored, and then when we got into all those old bones and things—it used to make me sick, kind of scare me. Chemistry's not so bad that way, anyway."

"Well, with your skin and feeling the way you do about old bones, maybe you'd better think twice before popping out to a dig in the western sunshine. At least at Beemeadows there's plenty of shade and the bones are all brand new."

She had succeeded; hating her own brutality, Helen pressed on quickly now that she had the girl's full, if horrified, attention. "Was Channing all right, Katey, when you left him on Tuesday? You were probably the last person to see him alive, you know—was he feeling okay, or acting strange? Don't worry, Louisa doesn't have to know a thing about it, and she certainly won't hear a word from me—I couldn't care a hoot about that end of it, it's none of my business, but—"

\*

Simon, carrying his own disposable lighter in his hand, came down into the barroom after what seemed a decent interval; the harpist had stopped playing in her corner and Helen was being hovered over by the bartender, who was wielding a towel over the littered tabletop, sweeping broken glass into a dustpan. Helen was mopping the remains of cream off her face, the lap of her dress, ignoring the stares of the few other customers.

"That's the last of *that* kid, lady—I sure am sorry, can I bring you another drink, you and the gentleman?"

"No, no, it's all right—my fault entirely; we both know her slightly and I think I just said something that rubbed the wrong way, you mustn't blame her, she's been having a rough time the last few days. Please."

"Well, if the boss hears she threw a drink in a customer's face—I sure don't know."

"Don't tell him. Simon, we'd better be off now, leave a nice tip for Katey, will you? One good turn deserves another."

"Well, I was thinking I'd rather have an Irish coffee than a brandy alexander, and I sure as hell got one," Helen laughed as Simon headed the car out of Great Bedford on the dark road back to Chetford.

"What was that all in aid of, if I may ask?"

"You may. . . . It occurred to me that Katey was probably the last person to see Channing alive, and I wanted to know if he'd been okay, so I asked."

"Just like that, outright? Oh, Helen."

"I know, but I just didn't feel like beating around the bush and I'm no good at it anyway."

"And?"

"Poor kid—embarrassed as hell I knew about her and Channing fooling around, of course. She didn't say a thing about how *he* was, but I did learn something—"

"Yes?"

"Thyroid or anemia or whatever, that girl's not just a bored and blah beauty, she's capable of a great deal of nice, healthy, murderous anger, she is."

"And you're wondering if she took a scunner to Channing that day?"

"Yep. That's exactly what I'm wondering."

*

"Beemeadows Farm." Helen lurched to the wall telephone in the office and leaned against the doorjamb, picking up the receiver. "One moment please" crackled dimly from the operator, the line buzzed enough to hold promise the connection might be made, whoever it was that was calling.

Simon had disappeared with the car first thing this morning, cross as a bear with a sore head, telling her to get her own breakfast, refusing any company or any shopping lists even though Helen was out of talcum powder to squirt down her cast to stop the itching, for one thing. To hell with him. The weather breeder of the day before had disappeared, as if charmed away by a beneficent night fairy with a magic wand, and the still-dry mown hay was being baled into hefty rectangles out in the meadows. Ada had apparently proved her prowess to herself sufficiently with the mowing machine; only Judah was working the co-op crew this morning, looking as haggard as any two-hundred-pound square-faced weather-beaten fortyish-and-some-year-old can when he's been jilted by a college girl. At least he had the sense to know the thirty miles between Chetford and the Black Griffon Inn were light-years and not miles, for the purpose of trying to see Katey again. Not dumb twice, Judah. Well, we all have our egg-on-the-face moments, Helen thought. She'd been cleaning up breakfast dishes when he came rattling up in the truck early this morning, and she'd passed on Katey's only message to him, about the garbage cans at the cabin. Ada must have told him earlier when she opened the store that Katey had left; his thundercloud face had only darkened a bit more.

The telephone crackled again, clicked, the line cleared. "Hello, Beemeadows," Helen repeated.

"Oh—oh. This is the Bayard Foundation calling, Miss Grace Wilber, could I speak to Mrs. Adaams, please?"

"I'm sorry, Miss Wilber. Mrs. Adaams is still away; this is Helen Bullock, could I take a message?"

"Oh, *dear*." Helen wondered if one could truly hear a damp Kleenex over a telephone and decided one could. "Well, Mr. Adaams' associates here at Bayard need to know about the funeral arrangements. Mrs. Hayward said when she was here first thing this morning she didn't know what had been decided and hoped Mrs. Adaams was at the farm by now. I wonder if you'd be good enough to have someone let us know; Mr. Adaams' closer colleagues and I would like to come up for the service if it's appropriate—"

"Surely, Miss Wilber, the minute anything's decided I'm sure Louisa will call you. By the way, I thought Mrs. Hayward was going to be with Webby's therapist this morning—if she's still there could you connect me? Mr. Giffard wanted her to bring back some things for him and he's afraid she'll forget."

"Oh, I think she said *Mr.* Hayward was with Webby; she had a *long* meeting with Mr. Mortimer and just left, Miss—"

"Bullock. Okay, thanks anyway."

"Miss Bullock, do you have any idea where Mrs. Adaams *is?* It seems so dreadful not to be able to send her my condolences; such a lovely lady and so gracious to us all during Mr. Adaams' years here."

"I wish we did, Miss Wilber, we all feel the same way." Poor gal; if ever she'd heard an office-wife touch it was that, especially the genuine respect and admiration for all she could not have been and never could be: Louisa herself.

She sagged back in the swivel chair, running a bent coat hanger down her cast to scratch. Weeks more before it came off. God, what a dump this office is—everything nobody else wanted or replaced with something better. The very thought of office work depressed Helen anyway, she'd avoided it all her life, even during her most desperate days, whether or not it involved Barcelona chairs or cast-off mission oak.

Good old Sally, right on the spot. Simon had told her of the "alarum bells from within letter" Miss Wilber had sent to Channing; Sally wasn't missing a moment now to insert Webster into the now empty consultative slot at the Bayard Foundation. From whence, if Webster was equal to keeping his head above water there, Sally would—through him—come to judge the quick and the dead if she had her way.

Really, Simon cross was absolutely impossible. I'm a sore head about a lot of things myself, I know, she thought, swiveling back and forth and working the coat hanger farther down, but I let it out and it's over. He's so effing polite all the time it seems twice as bad, thrice as bad when he does show a crack in his composure. Makes me wonder if he really is just putting up with me, *faute de mieux*.

If what he really wants is some nice self-contained lady like Louisa, I'd better make tracks now; that's not me, never was, can't be. I'd much rather go it again alone than feel as if I were a stone in his shoe. My own fault, really—I guess I've always flung myself at him when and where we could get together; maybe he's just been too well bred to say "no thanks."

When and where we could get together—few and far between so far. Maybe I really want it that way too. It's a hell of a lot easier playing *Private Lives* than *Who's Afraid of Virginia Woolf*, that's for sure. Need it be Coward *or* Albee, though? That's what you're really afraid of—that it might work out at all. Oh, heaven, heaven—she'd gotten the coat hanger down to the arch of her foot where the itch was. To hell with Father Simon Bede and the talcum powder. She scratched away blissfully, without him. Just as he hadn't said where he was going or why, so he hadn't said when he'd be back. Humph.

Still, she could hardly wait to tell him about Louisa's savings bankbook. Ray had come in earlier looking for the installation manual for the Adaamses' water heater; the new coil had finally come. They'd fumbled through the files, found the drawer with the Adaamses' personal papers. Ray had gone away in a happy trance, flipping through the manual, and left Helen sitting looking at a small green deposit book from a bank in Lee. "Payable to Channing Adaams and/or Louisa Anstruther Adaams." The account had been opened three years ago; must be for income tax, Helen thought, going through the blurred carbon copies of cashier's checks made out to the Internal Revenue Service four times a year. They would pay estimated tax quarterly, Channing being more or less "self-employed" for tax purposes. Helen sighed, wishing she had a Louisa in her life to do that sort of task for her. Every withdrawal was matched up with the carbon copies of the checks folded in the back of the book.

Except the last withdrawal, three weeks ago. There was no copy of a check for it at all, and it was for a wildly dissimilar sum, twenty-five hundred dollars. A lot to carry around in cash. For either of them.

# CHAPTER VIII

"Colonel Bemis? Simon Bede." The man behind the door managed to relax without losing his straight-backed military bearing, although when he opened the door and let Simon into the narrow hall, Simon saw the gray in his hair and skin wasn't due only to seeing him first through the screen door. Shut in, and it doesn't suit him.

"Come on in, Simon, glad to meet you." The man's handshake was firm, brief. "You'll have to give me a minute to finish with Dad—he's having a bad day." Bemis showed Simon into a box of a front room, dark and stifling from the overhanging roof of a sagging front porch that was too narrow to hold a chair unless one turned it sideways, thus giving the sitter a view of identical cramped front porches running side by side to either end of the block. But even if the porch had been deeper, one would only see the same thing across the street. It was a block among dozens of other blocks that could have been painted only by Edward Hopper, sad asphalt shingle façades, cracked sidewalks providing the only greenery as irrepressible weeds pushed up through the gaps in the concrete.

Simon heard Bemis's quick, neat steps going up the narrow stairs just inside the front door, move about overhead. "Charleeene!" The screen door to the other half of the house banged, Simon looked out the window, saw an upholstered slattern in a housedress leaning over the rail of her half of the porch. A child with a rusty red wagon draggled down the sidewalk. "Waddya doin'? Come git yer lunch before 'The Secret

Storm.'" Charlene picked her nose, slowly pulled the wagon up the wooden steps, went inside. Thin walls; Simon could hear the television in the neighbor's living room. Someone named Myrna was confiding in Anthony about Elizabeth's daughter's abortion; Ross had bungled it, of course; for a moment Simon thought he was losing his mind as the use of "the more absorbent paper towel" was recommended. A commercial, he hoped. Yes, Myrna was back now, answering the chimes of her doorbell, uneasily admitting Godfrey's first wife, Annette, who had decided to take dear Jeffrey's advice and plead *nolo contendere* to the district attorney's charge of drunken driving. It went on at an unbelievably slow pace, each actor seeming to need long lapses of silence before delivering their lines, as if to give them weight and import. Suddenly the sound switched to the rattle-tattle of animated cartoon music, there was the sound of a swift slap, Charlene's scream, Myrna was back yet again—Simon turned his ears off as best he could.

A sagging armchair covered in hopeless blue, scratchy upholstery decades ago, a matching sofa, linoleum-tile floor with a cheap imitation oriental rug, garish even in its grime. A framed picture of an Elks' gathering, an ancient cabinet-model radio near the armchair. A venetian blind over the window; the lighter color of gray paint on either side showed where curtains had once hung on wooden rings that were pushed to either side of the wooden pole over the window now. A beautiful table by the chair, rosewood adaptation of Queen Anne, Simon remembered Bemis was having some success in retirement as an *ébéniste*. He picked up the chess pieces, lying on the top, smiled.

Channing, unmistakably, the king, his vigorous hair springing from the grain of the wood. Louisa, the queen; Bemis was jolly good, he'd found just the bit of wood grain to suggest the white plume in her dark hair. Perce as a bishop! Delightful! The other must be Scott, he didn't recognize the face.

The knights, Ray Russell and Bemis himself, of course. Brilliant; Ada and Thelma strong, broad-sweeping rooks.

"I was working on those when you called from Pittsfield this morning; give me the opinion of a fresh Beemeadows eye —likenesses all right?" Bemis had come down, was in the kitchen drying his hands.

"Amazing. They're devilishly good—what about the pawns?"

"I thought woodchucks, they're typical of the farm even if you can't push 'em around pawnwise. You haven't met the Scotts, I guess, they look so much alike—you know how married people do after a long time sometimes—I put 'em both together opposite Perce. Hope they won't mind."

"Should think they'd be as honored as everyone else; it's really a beautiful piece of work."

"Thanks; it's sure as hell saved my life this summer, having something to keep busy with that could be interrupted—just sold two, the regular Staunton classics of course. Too bad in a way; I could have gotten a little more with boards to match, but I need my shop in the barn to do those. Come on in the kitchen; I've got us a sandwich lunch if that's okay. Nurse only comes twice a week now."

Simon mentally kicked himself as he and Bemis sat down at the chipped enamel table where two places were neatly set; should have thought to bring something, some of the Vermont loot, something from Thelma's garden. But he hadn't thought of Bemis as being so available until he had finished his quick errand early this morning in Pittsfield; he'd swung onto the turnpike on an impulse, stopping to telephone halfway through the drive over.

"This is very good of you, Colonel; I'll be glad to stand a watch if you need to go out." Bemis poured beer, passed mustard sandwiches.

"Thanks, let's eat and I'll see—it's tricky to tell when he's going to need me these days."

"No progress, I take it?"

"Depends on what you call progress." The tall, grizzled man's jaw chewed methodically. "He's dying, of course. No question about that. And I admit I've been thinking since Thelma called me last week if Channing weren't the luckier of the two. Going out in full parade, quick and fast. Never knew what it was to be really sick, never even had his appendix out. Oh, I know there's a school of thought that postulates spiritual benefits and growth in a long death, and I can't quarrel with it, but Dad's so far beyond that now—"

"Coma?"

"Wish that were it. I know he does, too. Pain. The most obscene four-letter word of them all when it's like it is with Dad. P-A-I-N. Nonstop. Tough old bugger, though, still clinging to Mary Baker Eddy; have to tell him the shots I'm giving him every four hours are vitamins. He'd bust a gusset if he knew they were morphine. I've got an old army buddy on my side here in the hospital, doctor, he gets it for me. Between him and the practical nurse—Dad thinks she's a 'cleaning lady'—hell, in a way she is, all either of us can do is keep him clean, the morphine's not working much any more—I suppose we're doing as much as a hospital could do. In this country, at least. Understand England's a little more realistic and uses heroin there when things get to this stage."

"Yes, I believe we do. Marijuana as well; it seems to eliminate most of the nausea after radiation therapy."

"Hmm. Well, even if Dad had permitted that, which of course he didn't, he's long past that. Hasn't eaten in God knows how long. Starving to death, essentially." Bemis got up for another beer; Simon hadn't realized how hot it was in the dreary little kitchen until a draft of cold air from the refrigerator found its way to his cheek. "Did you find out what Louisa was doing in Albany, by the way? And how's she holding up? Silly question, really. Like a rock, I'm sure." Bemis's knuckles, holding the beer bottle as he divided the contents between their two glasses, were white; there was a curious grim note in his voice—almost sarcastic, Simon thought, if that were possble.

"That's particularly why I came over to see you today; Louisa hasn't returned yet and no one's been able to reach her." He quickly filled the Colonel in on what he knew a little of from Ray's telephone call on Saturday—the last few days of search and supposition, the bus tickets to Albany, and Sally Hayward's irresponsible hypothesis, which seemed, now that he'd seen Bemis's circumstances, as unrealistic and improbable as the soap operas going on next door.

Bemis smiled wryly, took a drink of beer. "Stupid woman, Sally Hayward. I suppose I should be flattered. Well, she'll never win any ribbons for perception. No, I tried all the hotels, motels, so on for Ray first thing when he called me, even the hospitals—perhaps that was a bit dramatic, but —well, as you see, I've more time than anything else and I tried to imagine what she'd come here for in the first place; awful hole, Albany. Not that discomfort or lack of aesthetics ever have stopped the stalwart Louisa from a project. Half the people who know her think she's a martyr and the other half, a saint. Excuse me." A bell, sounding as if it belonged to a kitchen timer, went off in the room above the kitchen; Bemis crumpled his paper napkin into a ball, threw it into a wastebasket, and moved quickly up the stairs.

Almost before Simon had time to harden his conviction that it had indeed been sarcasm and an unrelieved bitterness in Bemis's voice each time he'd spoken of Louisa, Bemis's voice called down the stairs:

"Bede, up here please, on the double."

The stifling back bedroom stank of rotting tissues, dying flesh that, with any decency, should have been underground long since feeding worms and maggots rather than devouring itself so agonizingly, cell by cell. Bemis was fiddling with an intravenous drip leading to the arm of the man on the rented hospital bed; Simon could see only the tubes going into the body, coming out, the inverted glass bottle of sustenance above the head of the bed, the bag of murky yellow urine hanging below the mattress at the foot.

"Tried to turn over, pulled out the needle—" Bemis motioned Simon to the other side of the bed; together they lifted the old man, whose look itself was a silent scream, back into the middle of the bed. In spite of the synthetic fleece pad beneath him, the bed sores were appalling.

"Look, if you really have half an hour, I'm almost out of IV needles and used the last disposable diaper just before you got here—he won't need anything you'd be able to give him, just be here to see he doesn't thrash too hard—that bed's sides collapse when you look at them sometimes." He tapped the nearly empty intravenous bottle, put the kitchen timer on the dresser. "Well, he got most of it anyway, I'll be back soon."

The front door closed crisply; Simon sat in a straight chair by the one window; a small electric fan on the floor stirred the air. A noise from the bed; Simon got up, leaned over. The old man's face was surrounded by an aureole of white hair; he had not been shaven for a very long time. "Don't touch—don't touch—" he managed to whisper.

"Of course not, sir." Nor had Bemis touched him more than necessary, Simon thought, noting the beard and the long, gnarled toenails on the thin gray foot that had freed itself from the sheet, the fingernails of a mandarin on the old hand scarred and bruised with needle punctures. "Your son's gone to the drugstore; I'm Simon Bede, a friend from Beemeadows. Alf will be back directly."

The rheumy old eyes blinked once, closed. "No friend—none friend—evil—all you evil—will smite you as He has smitten me—saw it years ago, years—thought Army would—viper clever viper—no scandal but I saw him years ago—no friend, evil evil—all you, cursed and damned as he, mark of—" Simon backed away from the bed, hoping his absence would ease the old man's passion which was spewing out in a terrifying, expensive whisper. The breath of life, Simon thought, the breath of life, not meant to be squandered in hatred at the end.

He stood in the doorway, looking across the short dark hall into the front bedroom, feeling the sweat run down the back of his already soaked cotton shirt. He could see the end of a cheap pine bedstead, a discolored floor where once a rug had been, the end of a heavy table with a few tools on it. Bemis must work up here, then, to hear his father better. The long, broiling days upon days; it must seem to Alf that the planet never turned, that this time would not end.

The old man fell quiet; Simon moved across the hall to catch a less foul whiff of air from Alf's window. There were the beginnings of the black chessmen roughed out in chunks of rosewood on the worktable; Simon smiled at a nearly finished pawn, the little woodchuck's wringing hands and eager teeth happy to go anywhere, do anything. Three blond wood pieces stood out from the others; Simon, always interested in the complex and inexplicable standards and visions of perfection that caused artists to rework, discard, achieve another and higher culmination of their intention, picked one up, examined it, raised the other two from the table with reluctant astonishment, the pit of his stomach curdling.

A clank from the back room brought him to the moment; he quickly returned to the dying father, who had kicked one feeble foot against the restraining sides of the bed and knocked it down. Simon raised it, locked it back in place, eased the foot gently back onto the bed. "Don't—filth—don't touch—" The passion would not end, the malevolent eyes glared upwards now, straight at Simon. The "filth" and refusal to be touched were clearly not references to old Mr. Bemis's own condition and pain; in his mind it was Simon who bore that stigma. "—viper to my bosom—will not vow change or repent—flaunts you here before me—I curse you and him—as God destroyed Sodom you shall be destroyed—and he my son with you all his whores—"

"That'll do, Dad." Bemis stood in the doorway, parcels in his arms. His face told nothing; his father's own stations of the cross were clearly as familiar to the son as to the father. "Thanks, Bede, hope everything went well." He began automatically filling a syringe, looking at the clock on the wall, as his father hissed "—dare you now first time bring one here—," gently swabbed the old arm, inserted the needle, pushed the plunger down slowly.

Alf shook his head at Simon's offer of help, pantomimed out of the old man's line of sight, motioned him downstairs. Simon methodically rinsed off the sandwich plates, put condiments in the refrigerator, wiped the table, returned to the living room. Myrna and Anthony and Annette had been replaced in the adjoining living room with some sort of mad, spendthrift game show; someone was being forced to decide whether to settle for the snowmobile or take a plunge into the unknown and what lay behind some sort of veil.

"Sorry about that, he doesn't often talk at all any more." Bemis came in, carrying a wastebasket full of crumpled paper, redolent of the sick room upstairs. "Generally try to give him a sponge-off after his shot this time of day; is there anything particular you can think of I can help with about Louisa? Of course I'll call right off if I think of anything, but as of now—"

"No, I'm sure you've done all you could and we'll keep on grubbing; very decent of you to give me lunch, Alf; let me know if you need another breather, I'll be delighted to come back."

"Thanks. It was easier up until this month, I could have the nurse oftener, but as you see, I don't think it'll be much longer. Tomorrow, the day after—" Bemis held open the screen door, lit a cigarette, looked up the empty street quivering in the sun, detaining Simon on the porch by a casual slouching against the doorjamb that ill-became his former upright bearing. "Well, I'm sorry again he was so garrulous; don't know what brought that on, he hasn't said a word for about ten days."

"It's not uncommon toward the end for that to happen, you know—a sprint of consciousness, so to speak. Heard many a confession that way, sacramental or temporal, and I've come to think those I've been with who were given that last bit of energy died more quietly, easily. They'd emptied themselves, as it were."

"Hmm. I forgot you were a priest; you'd know more than I about that end of it—" Bemis flicked his cigarette out into the gutter. Sensing the man's self-torment behind the relaxed pose and masklike face, Simon suddenly thought of Helen and how, if she were about to do what he had to do now, she would cross her fingers behind her back.

"In any event, Alf, whatever it was that was on his mind—couldn't understand a word of it, of course, wish I could be of help and give you a hint, but his voice is so frail and the telly from your neighbor—but indeed, whatever it was *is* off his chest, which is the important thing. I'm sure you'll find him easier in spirit."

"Yes." Bemis straightened, looked up and down the street, at Simon. "Yes, I hope so. A lot of disappointments in his life; be good if he came to terms with things at last. Very little I can do to help him."

Very little, Simon thought, looking at the man's prison pallor, the ovenlike house ready to grasp him the moment Simon left, the decades of confused anger and guilt that had brought Bemis back here to see that his father was allowed to die the way he wished, since the son could live only the way he was made. Not so very little to do, a very great deal.

"Keep fit yourself," the jolly, hollow parson's words rang out, embarrassing them both. "Look forward to seeing the chess set when it's finished, it's a fine piece of work."

"Say, I'd rather that was a surprise for when I come back

to the farm if you don't mind—besides, it may be some time before it's done; with Channing dead it's rather hard—"

"Of course." Simon deliberately misinterpreted Bemis's meaning. "But you'll be able to spot the time when Louisa'll be able to see it for the beauty it is instead of a painful reminder, I'm sure."

"Oh, yes. Louisa." The screen door next to Bemis slammed, Charlene dragged herself out, picked up the handle of the red wagon. After shaking hands quickly with Bemis, Simon scorched his hands on the steering wheel of the car, which had been baking in the sun for what seemed to him an eternity.

*

"Hello there, Simon! Tell me something—is there a worse time of day than late afternoon on a Monday?" Thelma sat back on her heels in front of Louisa's open icebox, surrounded with souring quarts of milk, a garbage bag full of slimy vegetables, a saucepan full of water and baking soda.

"Yes, there is. Monday noon in Albany." Simon lolled against the Adaamses' kitchen wall, looking exhausted and very much at loose ends to Thelma as he told her of his impromptu visit to Alf Bemis.

"Oh, dear, was it as drab as that? I must go over and give him a breather again; I was there several times earlier and at least it was cool—that horrid little house would be a sweatbox on a day like today. Poor Alf, he's such a staunch son; frankly I think the old man would have adjusted quite quickly to a hospital or, better yet, being here; dying people just have to and they seem to know it, but Alf—well, honestly, I don't think it's the stoic soldier bit, he's not like that at all, but it's as if he were determined to pay back some impossible debt, or punish himself for something, letting that old man put him through months of this. And of course he won't borrow a penny from any of us, he used to be able to get over here for a lunch or just a ramble when the nurse came for longer, or meet Ray and me at Tanglewood—we missed him yesterday." She wiped the perspiration off her forehead, peered into the refrigerator. "There, the rest of those things, cheese and salami and stuff'll keep—they're meant to stink. I'll put the butter in the freezer so it doesn't soak up the smell."

She stood up, poured the dirty water down the drain, rinsed the pan. "God, that's cold. Ray's furious with me." She grinned at Simon, handing him a welcome glass of cold tap water. "He has the new coil for Louisa's hot-water heater, and Helen found the installation manual for him down in the office this morning. He was all set to come up and have a field day putting it in, but I got ahold of him first—can you imagine, I was vacuuming the living room in our house this morning and a *bat* flew right out of the fireplace at me! You should have seen me, swatting at it with the hose from the vacuum and trying to wrap up my hair in a kerchief at the same time —I know"—she laughed at herself—"they don't *really* aim for your hair, but—anyway, Ray's been up on our roof fixing the chimney-pot screens instead, and if I know him he's probably decided to clean the chimney while he's at it—I shudder to think what I have to go home to, soot all over the living room, no doubt. Well, better than having him electrocute himself, he was all for trying to put the new coil in without the manual but I made him find it."

"Louisa doesn't keep a desk up here, then?"

"No, she has to spend so much time down in the office anyway she found it was simpler to keep their personal papers down there too; I guess the only things up here are Channing's business files and all." She squeezed out a sponge, turned off the water. "Oh, drat, these must have just been rinsed—they're all greasy."

She had started to put away the breakfast and lunch dishes stacked in the drainer, held one up to the light. "Well, with only the spring water they would be—my hands are numb from it now." She turned on the electric burner under the teakettle, sighing.

Simon wandered mousily back into Channing's den; the place was like an oven with the curtains drawn back and the late sun glaring through the double-glass walls and sliding door. The potting wheel was caked white with dried clay; it was hot enough in that corner for it to be a virtual kiln itself. Simon idly pressed the electric switch with his toe, the wheel revolved swiftly, spinning fine white powder out centrifugally. He lifted his toe, it stopped. If Channing had been potting, and he had, he wouldn't have left the piece on the wheel in that sun—he'd have draped it heavily with wet cloth and plastic, or better, put it back in the wet cupboard. Left out to bake like that, it would have dried far too fast for a careful potter, it would have been—amateurish. Channing was not that.

He sat down at the desk, revolving in the swivel chair, sour even to the beauty of the room. He contrasted it in his mind with the office Louisa worked in, a fuggy hole of a hall bedroom probably intended for a hired hand or impoverished relation, one stuffy window with the view and air blocked by a dying lilac tree planted too close to the house. An ancient typewriter, adding machine, rows of neat ledgers and deed boxes full of the community's records of expenditures, income, tax forms. A huge institutional calendar on the wall by the telephone, a slate with chores to be done chalked up, hooks for keys to cars, houses, cupboards. Leftovers, the roll-top desk and splintered chair, khaki goose-neck lamp. There was a piece of old linoleum on the floor.

He reached out one hand and flipped on the switch to Channing's electric typewriter, switched off the low, expensive hum. Quite a difference. An electronic calculator, white push-button telephone, digital clock and calendar. Simon looked at the wall masking the storage cupboards, files, and

wet-clay cupboard. A sample of the best of each of his hob-
bies, Channing had said. A trout fly in a shadow-box frame, a
glass case of exotic butterflies, another of shells, a rather good
photograph of the main Beemeadows house with an electric
storm coming up, lightning crackling in the sky. A framed
postage stamp, an old photograph of a ruefully laughing, very
young Channing, still in navy uniform, one arm in a sling and
the other jokingly holding a pistol at the motor of a smashed-
up motorcycle. Simon squinted at it—he'd seen that background. Ah, yes. Brand's Hatch. So he'd gone in for racing
after the war, or at least enough to give it up with a broken
arm or collar bone.

"Can you give me a ride down, Simon? I'm through here, I
think everything'll hold together for a while now—" Thelma
came in briskly, as always sweeping away cobwebs of depres-
sion with her sheer abundance of health and sanity. "What
are you looking at me like that for?"

"Was I? Sorry." Something in Simon yearned, broke. "I was
thinking how all this week I'd been missing something I
didn't know I was missing, didn't know I wanted. You and
Ray have it, Channing and Louisa have—had—it. The Scotts,
I assume. The two by two. Being north on each other's
compasses."

"You were married, weren't you? I've heard you speak of
your son."

"Yes, Fergus, great chap. He's in his mid-twenties now,
crashing his huge hulk about trying to make a niche in the
film business one way or another. Anthea, his mother, died in
an auto smash when he was fifteen."

"What was she like?"

"To look at? Fair, small, English to the core—Fergus gets
his color and frame from my bit of Welsh and his American
grandmother. Like otherwise? Loyal. Organized. Unresentful.
Too many of our years together weren't together at all; I was
traveled unmercifully, rushed in and out of Lambeth for years

to one spot or another—Anthea never had a chance to be the parish priest's wife she'd expected to be; she'd have done it brilliantly and happily, the dear, she had all the accomplishments for it. Just her cup of tea."

The digital clock clicked, Thelma dabbed at her perspiring upper lip with a dustcloth. "Someone once said all love has to end in unhappiness one way or another, unless both die at exactly the same time in each other's arms. I think that's probably true. But I do get so cross with people who say 'I don't know what I'd do without so-and-so' or 'I couldn't live without him or her.' Ray and I are like a pair of bedroom slippers, I know, but I also know that if I had to, or he had to, go on alone, we'd manage perfectly well somehow. People do. Alf Bemis, for instance—well, of course that's different. But Perce survives quite well, don't you think, and Ada, even though she has the sense to hanker after Judah, seems to be biding her time quite triumphantly, or maybe just gallantly. You don't seem to be doing so badly yourself, so far as I can see." She looked thoughtfully at his profile, the woods and rocks beyond he was looking toward.

"Mmmm. But I've been wondering if it isn't—I always thought it was because of myself that I went on; now I'm wondering if it isn't in spite of myself."

"High time. You have a very good thing between you and Helen—a comfortable flow of attention and a lot of—well, humor."

"Indeed we do. When we have world enough and time to be together I feel—finished, complete. And yet she is so utterly complete herself, without me, and always has been. And on top of it all, I've now dragged her into this mess up here— *not* a holiday at all."

"Nonsense." Thelma snapped the dustcloth at him. "You're indulging yourself, Simon. She adores you to the better-or-worse point, just as you do her. Sheer havering, as you English say, on your part. Nobody's complete, not since Noah launched his Ark. Come on, I want to get some cheap beer down at the store to put out for the slugs this afternoon; Perce has a fit if I use his Guinness and he's right. And, dread it as we do, the Haywards are coming back this afternoon. I hope Dr. Blanford was some help." She looked out at the deck; it was swept clean of the carpet tacks now, but the rusty pocks remained, freckles of death.

"Terribly hot in here but I suppose we'd better close up tight." She reached behind the pulled-back curtains, slid the glass door across from one wooden jamb to another, a string of butterfly decals on it just at chest height alone revealing that the door had been open all along, not closed as Simon had thought. Sally had said it had been closed when she came up for the directory that day.

Thelma was waiting for Simon, her arms full of trash bags, by the front door. He was gazing at the South American artifacts over the fireplace, the ritual masks with their pounding combination of primal and sophisticate, the fine delicate basketwork. He reached up for a little quiver, turned it over, rehung it. "Helen said I'd mishung that—what were you saying, Thelma?"

"I was wondering what we should do about that bowl that Sally brought down Tuesday with Channing's directory; she put it down in the cellar by the kiln. But I don't suppose any of us know enough about firing—well, Louisa can decide. Simon, where the hell *is* she? Ray didn't tell you and Helen and me yesterday; he only admitted it when we were getting ready for bed last night. The ticket to Albany Louisa bought was just one-way. All the others had been round-trip, but the last one was one-way."

# CHAPTER IX

"Comfortable?" Simon came up the outside cellar stairs by the back porch, carrying cartons of canning jars for Perce, who was already filling the kitchen with agonizing aromas of raspberry and blackberry jam and jelly. Helen had been commandeered right after breakfast and put in an armchair with a bushel of string beans at one side, a paper bag at her feet, and a saucepan full of water at the other side. Thelma threatened at least another bushel to come; she was out picking early in the morning before the heat of the day took over.

"Yep. I find fixing these things is just about the same as cropping snapshots." She cut off both ends of a bean, sliced it diagonally in three pieces as Perce had instructed, and dropped it in the pan. "Who was it who had the unemptiable pitcher in Greek myths?" She looked tired, glowered at the bushel basket beside her.

"Baucis and Philemon," Simon said over his shoulder. "Dear old couple—hospitable to some visiting gods in disguise, who in return not only kept the wine flowing à la the wedding at Cana, but did Christ one better by granting them their wish to die together—turned them into sturdy old trees side by side with their branches fore'er entwined." I wonder if he's getting a cold, Helen thought, his voice sounds funny, thick.

"*Thought* you'd know," she said, a strange look on her face.

Simon put the preserving jars on the long kitchen counter

next to the scalded jelly glasses Perce had set out. "That do it, cuz?"

"Thank you kindly, Simon. Very good of Helen to take on the beans for me; she must take home several quarts to remember us by this winter." Simon forbore to tell Perce that an opened quart of green beans in Helen's refrigerator would collect more mold than happy memories; she seldom attempted to cook for herself or anyone else. A jar or two of jam would be a more practical souvenir.

"I'm going to be down at Ada's this morning—any odd bits you need? Shan't be back for a bit, however."

"Yes, a box or two of paraffin—white wax to you English. Thought I had enough from last year, but Thelma has a bounty crop of berries this year." Perce skimmed the simmering jelly thoughtfully, rapped the scum from his spoon into the sink, stirred.

Simon picked up a cloth-wrapped parcel he had brought up from the cellar with the jars and started up the stairs. Webster had not, after all, come back with Sally and Webby last night. "Business in the city, he'll come up on the bus tomorrow," Sally had said last night, trailing in with a tired, white Webby, who had been carsick twice on the trip up. The child had refused any dinner, sitting slumped in his chair, picking on his hangnails.

He was still in bed; Simon tiptoed in the open door of the boy's room, the floor littered with candy and gum wrappers, comic books, the child firmly asleep in spite of the clatter of Sally's typewriter. Escape, Simon thought, the best in the world, sleep. Except for dreams. He wished Webby well with his subconscious, laid a book of easy Bach piano duets that he'd found in Pittsfield yesterday on the foot of the bed, and went out closing the door behind him.

"Oh, Simon." Sally looked up distractedly, an easel behind her with a gigantic pad of graph paper shutting out the view from the window, the walls heavily thumbtacked with charts, outlines, notations.

"Shan't be a minute. I just need to know if this is what you brought down from Channing's last week when you went up for his directory."

"What? Is that Webster's T-shirt—I told him to bring the laundry up before we left." She scratched her head with a pencil, peered through thick-lensed glasses at the clay bowl Simon had unwrapped from the grayish undershirt. "Oh, yes, it was on the wheel and dry as a bone, I put it down by Channing's kiln for him. Webby hoped Channing'd be ready to fire some little bits of junk he'd made earlier, Channing was waiting to have a kiln full. They're all down there, but I suppose it's too late. Doesn't matter anyway, I'm sure Webby's forgotten about them."

Simon wondered if she'd ever looked at Webby's "little bits of junk"—very charming they were, squirrels, woodchucks, dogs, cats, a nesting bird.

"I see. I believe you said the house was all closed—not locked, but closed, the door to the deck and all?"

"Of course—what I saw of it, just went right into the den and back out, but it was hot as the devil in there with the glass walls."

"Yes, I was up there yesterday with Thelma about the same time of day. I thought the door was closed myself, but it was open after all—as we left Thelma slid it closed and there's a line of butterfly decals across the door, probably to keep people from smashing into it, it's that nonreflecting glass that's so difficult to see. Did you notice the butterflies?"

"Good heavens, Simon, of course not. Far too busy—I just took the directory and the bowl and came right back. What *is* this all for, I'm really rushed this morning." And far too rushed then reading that letter from Grace Wilber that was on Channing's desk; Sally could hardly have missed seeing the

Bayard Foundation letterhead; it fairly leaped at you from the side of the desk the bookcase was near.

"Sorry. Good luck with the book." He left her bent over her typewriter, her oily short black hair wreathed in smoke from one of her mentholated, filtered cigarettes that was burning out malodorously in an overflowing ashtray. The cigarette on Channing's desk had been plain, unfiltered. Katey's brand.

Helen, snipping away at the beans, didn't seem to have made a dent in the bushel yet. Simon set the wrapped bowl down carefully behind him and pulled out his penknife, took a handful of beans.

"Anything besides talcum powder for you, love?"

"Nope." Actually, Ada had provided a better solution than coat hangers or talcum powder; she'd brought Helen over her hair dryer with the hose disconnected from the hood; set on "cool" with the hose stuffed in the top of the cast, it was sheer heaven. Damned if she'd tell Simon that, let him think she was suffering. "The *Times,* of course, if there's one. What's wrapped up in that rag?"

"No secrets from you, have I?" He smiled with his eyes.

Damn, Helen thought, savaging a bean into shreds, there I go again, pushing into his privacy. From now on I'll treat him like royalty, no direct questions. If Your Majesty wishes to tell me what is wrapped in that rag, I am all ears.

"This has to be quite *entre nous* for the moment, but I'll explode unless I can talk to you. Cross your heart?"

"And hope to die," she answered automatically, looking at him straight for the first time, seeing the tired lines around his eyes. She'd wakened once during the night, seen him sitting in the rocker by the window, looking out into the moonlight.

"I told you about seeing Alf Bemis yesterday." He fell silent, searching for something in his mind.

"In gory detail—poor guy, I can sympathize. As an advance penance for more sins than I can commit in a lifetime I once had to take care of an old lady who hated my guts, everybody's guts, so at least it wasn't personal, but I was just a kid. It was hell. But there's Bemis, with his own father hating him for quite a specific reason—wonder the stray air bubble hasn't found its way through the hypodermic needle. Alf must be a hero."

"More likely, atoning."

"How d'you mean—Alf's generation's guilt and self-hatred for not being cut out of the same cookie cutter everybody else is and liking men instead of women? Well, he's playing a mug's game; living or dying he'll never make it up to a father like that and he might as well get on with the business of enjoying himself; he's bound to be a hell of a nice guy, everybody here says he's terrific."

"And will be again when he gets back here for good—but at the moment—d'you remember the chess set I told you of? As a secret?"

"Sure. I wish I could see it—I love his perception of Thelma and Ada as the rooks—*vive* women's lib!"

Simon smiled and squeezed her hand. "Glad you see his admiration for them in giving them those pieces, they had genuine feeling, all of them. It's the ones upstairs that trouble me."

"Upstairs?"

"Yes, in his bedroom—his carving table is there. You aren't the only one who goes through medicine chests. There were roughed-out starts for the blacks in rosewood, but also on the table were three different blond pieces—I thought them rejects from the finished set downstairs at first, but they weren't. You asked me about Baucis and Philemon a bit earlier; these were mythological in a sense as well—I hope not legendary—they were finished, finely finished, Channing as king, but you could tell only by the crown. The rest was

Channing adapted to Michelangelo's 'David,' stockier of course but the same tantalizing stance. Alf as knight, but this time an extremely priapic centaur—no need for a lance, I assure you. There was something hideous in those two faces—Channing's magnificent head cocked in a sort of sublime tease, Alf's riddled with lust."

"And the third piece?"

"Louisa. Nude again, as the other two, with hollowed belly and shriveled breasts, everything lean and fine, but thickened Medusa's serpents for hair."

"Her face?"

"A skull. Just a skull."

"Whew! Talk about sticking pins in wax dolls—what d'you think, Simon?"

He hugged his arms across his chest, looked out across the lawn. "I don't know—I know what I *want* to think is that a distressed, overextended and yet compressed-by-circumstances man has been shut up too long in a hot box of a house with a hateful task to perform for a hating father, whose approval he would love but knows he'll not ever have. I want to think the loneliness and heat and stress and boredom have encouraged his kinks—which I doubt are any kinkier than yours and mine —to fester out of all proportion, producing a blond wood daydream, nightmare, fantasy all in one."

"You don't want to think maybe Channing, who heaven knows loved admiration, adulation, was onto Bemis's feeling for him and *was* playing a bit of a tease? Wouldn't put it past him, you know—he'd have seen it as an idle amusement and not given a thought to the cruelty to Bemis—and that Louisa maybe took it seriously and went over to Albany to beard the Colonel in his lair and is now lying chopped up in chunks in a trunk in the cellar?"

"Good God, woman, cutting up those beans has gone to your head," Simon groaned. "No, I *don't* want to think that but I confess it's in my mind as a hideous possibility. It's also in my mind that perhaps—just perhaps—" He broke off a twig of dead lilac, snapped it into small pieces.

"Yeah, perhaps Bemis came over to get a glimpse of Channing—with or without an invitation—Albany's not that far away and you say he still does have a practical nurse *once* in a while—he could have buzzed over last week, probably just hoping to chew the fat if Channing were at home, and if not, come on down and see the others. And finding Channing, who had always seemed so godlike and true blue and unattainable to anyone but the formidable Louisa tussling in the sack with the first and easiest thing at hand, which happened to be little Katey, pulled out an emotional horsewhip and drove Channing over the edge of the deck out of jealousy and betrayal?"

"Helen, Helen—it's a script for a Joan Crawford movie, the whole ruddy thing."

"Well, hell, you've met the man and I haven't. I'm stuck here most of the time and don't know beans about him or anything *but* beans. I feel more like the sour green midget than the jolly green giant, I can tell you—if it weren't for this cinder block on my leg maybe you'd have taken me into Albany with you and I'd have a better idea of the guy himself; as I said, all I've heard is that he's likable, responsible, a pillar of the community, and everybody misses him a lot so he must have a lot going for him if people as diverse as Thelma and Perce and Ada and all agree about him."

Simon dropped the lilac twigs; Helen's neck and ears were red with anger, she was snapping beans furiously.

"Helen—"

"Hmm?"

"It wasn't your leg that kept me from taking you with me—I hated to get you more entangled in this mess here, you must know that. This is a rotten holiday for you, isn't it? We've no obligation, you know, we were only meant to take a tea off

Perce to satisfy Aunt Priscilla, and here you are with broken bones in the demanding and distracted company of mournful, distressed people who would, I'm sure, be delightful under other circumstances. But these circumstances *are* here. Shall we leave the beans and the berries behind us and make our way on to the Adirondacks?"

"Oh, for heavens sakes, Simon, you know perfectly well you wouldn't sleep a wink if you didn't know that Louisa were back and all right—neither of us would. The Adirondacks'll still be there—"

"I hadn't intended to inflict even a peripheral family stay on you—certainly not such a melancholy one."

"Ha. And here I'd been thinking you'd arranged it all with the travel agent. Well, don't you worry, buster, if it were my cousin I'd sure as hell suck you into it. For animal comfort, if nothing else."

"Sure?" He took her paring knife away, lifted her chin up, and forced her to look into his eyes.

Something was still withheld, but much had returned—much. He felt it in her kiss.

"Sure. Go on down and get Ada to put ten bucks on nine in the ninth for me today, will you?"

"Nine in the ninth. Ten dollars. Very well." He wrote it carefully next to "paraffin, Perce" on his list.

See, Helen said to herself, he doesn't ask *me* why or what. Or how I chose that horse—I don't even know where or what's running. What a hell of a great-looking backside he's got—Simon stood up and was brushing off the flaking paint from the veranda's steps.

"Helen, this has to stay very carefully and quietly in the care of the two of us." He picked up his ragged parcel. "Top of the highboy?"

"Why not."

He came out, car keys in hand. "Tell me, you said you'd

knocked over all those South American things I hung on the wall for Louisa—there must have been more than one of these in that little quiver, weren't there?"

"Hell yes, there were at least two dozen or more—I thought they were part of Webby's jackstraws at first, until I saw the ends."

On Simon's outstretched hand lay a slender, dry, dark-tipped sliver of wood, very like an attenuated jackstraw indeed except for the faded, brownish feathers on one end.

"Yes." He wrapped it carefully in his handkerchief. "I'll put it back where I found it then. On top of the highboy where Louisa put the baskets that morning. This must have snagged off one of them and she didn't see it. It's dark in that corner in the morning; I found it just now stuck in a crack in the top."

*

Really, Thelma thought, slashing a slug in two with her hoe as she saw Simon drive off toward Chetford, those two. Glum as the inside of an old thermos bottle at dinner last night. I suppose Beemeadows isn't the most romantic spot in the world just now, but still—something was out of kilter between them, different from the general gloom. Silly ass of a man; of course Helen was self-sufficient and independent, whatever *that* meant. In Thelma's mind what that meant was that Helen had simply done in her life what she had to do, and kept on being Helen. Which in no way meant that there wasn't plenty of room and plenty of need in her for Simon. How like a man not to see that—whatever else was she doing with him? A woman like that would have plenty of other things to do; couldn't he see Helen herself had chosen him, and not Helen's circumstances? Not because she *had* nothing better to do, but because there *was* nothing better to do than be with him?

Oh, lord, I put in too many tomato plants again this spring —Perce'll have a fit when they all come ripe at the same time; I'll have to smuggle some down to Ada to sell in the store if she can. Perce will never let me give him a hand canning.

\*

"Okay, Padre, your bet's on too—didn't know you played the horses." Ada came back to the counter from the telephone; Simon finished unpacking a carton of creamed corn and tossed the empty box into a pile by the door.

"I'm full of surprises. What time is it? Only ten?"

"Yep. Want a coffee? I usually do about now." He's jumpy as a cat, Ada thought, and what is he really doing down here anyway? She handed him a mug, pushed powdered cream, sugar at him, hooked another stool up behind the counter with one foot and sat down.

A station wagon pulled up in front of Judah's. A smart young mother in seventy-five-dollar blue jeans came in, followed by two tow-headed, quiet children. Four apples, a piece of cheese, a tin of dog food, two comic books. The screen door clicked politely as they went out. Ada heard the "ding" on Judah's gas pump as the tank was filled, the sound of the men's room door closing, the car doors being shut crisply, the woof of a dog, and off they drove. The morning crept on.

"Hey there, Simon." Judah ambled in, took a bag of potato chips, ripped it open with his teeth. "Keepin' store for Ada again?"

"No, she's in the back room."

"Hey, Ada!" Judah bawled. "Good news!" He was clean-shaven, his eyes bright, a faded but clean work shirt with the sleeves neatly rolled up to show his tattoo. The hangover, both alcoholic and emotional, was more or less out of his system, Simon was glad to see.

"What's good news? It isn't even post time at the track

yet." Ada came bustling out of the back room, a sheaf of papers in her hand.

"Don't you ever think about nothing but the horses? I got ahold of Marshall—turned ass over teakettle to be nice about getting together with Beemeadows for the zoning hearing just as soon as the funeral's over. Full of commiseration, respect, all that. You won't have any trouble now. When is the funeral, anyhow?"

"If I knew, or anybody did, we'd all be better off."

"No Louisa yet? Jeez, this is crazy."

"That's just the word for it. Don't know what you can tell Marshall, Judah, you might as well just name a night and Ray or I can show up easy, or Thelma or Perce. Only takes one of us anyway. We can at least get that string tied up; it'll make a nice homecoming present for Louisa if nothing else. You sure as hell look bright-eyed and bushy-tailed this morning, by the way."

"Yah? That's good. After actin' like a horse's ass for half the summer thought I'd better try and look like the other end for a change. Civic pride. Don't do to besmirch the fair name of Chetford by goin' around with my tail between my legs." He winked at Ada, grinned at Simon. "Come on, buy you both a beer. You look like you need one. Ada too. One of your nags come in last, kid?"

"As a matter of fact, I'm $84.50 ahead as of this week. That includes the telephone bill, too." Ada passed out beer, offered a bag of corn chips to Simon, who shook his head. "Gotta get over to the post office; Tuesday's the day my nephew's check comes. And as for our blackjack game, Judah, last time I looked you were $5,342 down."

"Hell, Ada, I ain't had my mind on it recently, but just you give me a chance and I'll be outa the hole in five hands. How about after you close up tonight?"

"You're on, big spender. Hey, Simon, listen for the phone and things, will you? I just want to nip across for the mail."

She came back thumbing through a sheaf of letters, sorting them out on the counter. "Russell, Russell, Perce, me, Perce, Scotts, Hayward, Hayward, Adaams, Hayward, Adaams. Okay, Simon, if I stick them in the grocery bag?" He nodded absently from the telephone in back, listening intently to the receiver. Ada tore open her own envelope, waved the check under Judah's nose.

"See, like I said. Old Cho-San pulled up in the stretch last Wednesday in the third just like I knew he would—great mudder, that horse, it was raining down there too like up here. Good news, Simon?"

Bede's back was straight, eyes snapping; the aura of irritable loose ends that had exuded from him all the long morning at the store had vanished as he came back down the crowded aisle of the little musty store, its floor redolent of sweeping compound.

"The best of news, the worst of news. But one person's going to have his life changed, thanks be to God."

"Who's that?"

Simon scooped up the grocery bag, dug the car keys out of his pocket excitedly.

"Not anybody's favorite, but more deserving than we know. In his own way a great little mudder too. Webby."

*

Simon came out of Webby's room and closed the door. He'd left the boy struggling excitedly into his shorts and a shirt, promising him an overdue breakfast and lunch in one—and a go at the duets with him tonight after dinner. The lad'd keep his word not to say anything yet, not that Simon had told him anything but what was essential for Webby to know to remove guilt and explain accidents. He hurried down to the kitchen to give Perce a hand with the boy's meal, found his cousin standing by the kitchen counter, the grocery bag empty, letters on the counter, and a vast kettle of jam boiling over on the stove. His shaking hand held a letter; the sounds coming from his mouth sounded as if his very soul were being torn quietly to bits.

Simultaneously turning out the fire under the jam and bracing an arm around Perce's shoulders, Simon saw the words and meaning of the letter jump out at him.

"Helen," he called firmly, "Helen." She stumped in as fast as she could, paring knife in hand, followed by Ray. "Helen, get your things, Perce's jacket—over there on the chair—Ray, give Webby a good feed, will you? He'll be down in a minute. Helen and I are taking Perce to Albany."

# CHAPTER X

The surgeon, Dr. Clement, slapped an X ray on a glass board, flipped on the light. Delicate bones, clearly defined, ribs, spine, collar bones—"This is her heart when she first came to me late in May, the twenty-ninth, I believe. You see the enlargement of the ascending arch, the aneurysm—here, compare it with a normal heart." Another X ray went up; the difference was dramatic. "A clear case then of extremely well-advanced syphilitic aortitis with imminently impending rupture even in May. Unfortunately Mrs. Meadows—sorry, Mrs. Adaams—waited two months; you see the rapid progress of the enlargement of the heart and the aneurysm here in this picture of a month ago and here, just before surgery last week." The aorta had enlarged so that the upper ribs were not visible at all, nor the spine; the heart was vast, enormous. "Although even in May, if she'd accepted my advice and had the surgery done immediately, her chances were extremely poor, extremely. And of course nothing much could have been done for the other damage, tabes dorsalis and so forth, even if she had lived; that was what brought her to me in the first place, told me she thought she had arthritis. Well, they're both hellishly painful and affect the joints, but that's about the only similarity. I had the feeling she knew, then, and was wanting me to confirm another doctor's diagnosis. Pity in a way the tabes dorsalis didn't show up years sooner—the heart surgery might at least have been successful then.

"And of course with such advanced tertiary syphilis I suspected a great deal more damage as well; after she died I had a look at the thoracoacromial aorta as well—more damage there. She was sterile, of course, that was from the gonorrhea, though—not an uncommon combination, unfortunately. Tubes and ovaries atrophied, adhesions, scarring. Said she'd been in South America out in a small jungle village about twenty-five years or so ago, alone, had a bout of what she thought was painful cystitis, that'd be the gonorrhea, of course, that lasted a day or so, drank lots of water, took a bit of sulfa, and rested, it went away. That was the only symptom, as is so often the case; the blasted things went quiet and lay low for decades until this spring, when it was too late.

"Curious woman; extremely self-contained even when I made it clear what slim chance she had. I suspected a false name when she insisted on making the entrance deposit here at the hospital in cash and paying me as well before the operation. However, with a patient like that one feels they're as entitled to as much privacy as we can give them. Sorry about the notification of her death going to Chetford, Maine, instead of Massachusetts, Mr. Giffard—when she listed you on the hospital form as next of kin her handwriting was rather deteriorated from drugs, the office did its best. I gather you would have been told sooner if she'd given us your telephone number; it's unlisted, I believe? So the letter was the best we could do."

\*

Someone had to satisfy the insurance and legal and filing requirements of the hospital, of course; Louisa had spared all of them all she could, but not identifying her body. Simon and Perce returned from the bowels of the hospital, meeting Helen at the cashier's office where she was taking care of bills, health insurance forms, receipts for Louisa's belongings. Might as well go through the whole whing-ding, Helen thought; Louisa and Channing had a major medical policy that should reimburse their estate for most of the expenses. Talk about straining at camels and catching gnats, she told herself as she stuffed the papers into her bag and took Perce's arm. Well, it's all any of us can cope with right now.

Simon picked up Louisa's elegant little canvas weekend bag with a green stripe around it, faint chalkings from far-off customs officers, a piece of hotel label. It was over.

*

"Here's her handbag, Perce. The nurse couldn't get it in the suitcase with the rest of her things." Helen remembered the quiet, stylish linen summer dress and jacket, the pumps Louisa had worn; the suitcase was small, she'd probably taken only a nightgown and robe. Knowing she'd need nothing more. Helen handed Perce the straw bag with the gold clip. "They asked me to look through it to see if everything was there before I signed a receipt; but God knows I haven't the faintest idea what she took—there's an envelope with your name on it, though."

Perce nodded, sitting upright in the back seat of the car, one hand on Louisa's little suitcase and the other stroking the straw handbag on his lap, gently and slowly.

"Thank you, Helen."

*

Miles later Simon realized none of them had eaten since breakfast at seven; he pulled onto the apron of a clean-looking diner, helped Helen out, led Perce to a formica and chrome booth. He was fully prepared to force-feed the old man some of the excellent vegetable soup and scrambled eggs and toast he'd ordered for them all. Perce, however, ate obediently, drank a cup of tea.

"Read the letter, Perce. Whatever is in it, it will make a

difference. I'm sure of it." Perce opened the handbag, which he had brought in with him and was still holding on his lap.

"Yes, yes I will." He took his glasses from the breast pocket of his crumpled linen jacket, opened the bag, and pulled out an envelope, slit it open. He unfolded and read the sheets of paper, his expression unchanging. He passed the letter to Simon, wiped his mouth carefully, got up and went out. They saw him through the window of the diner, sitting on a bench under a tree.

Dear Perce,

I am dead already as I write this for you. Channing killed me twenty-five years ago and the only thing I think is amazing now is that he had the time for it—how busy he always was. Dr. Clement will have told you, or will tell you, the things that can be told precisely, all the measurables and touchables and seeables. I hope you have someone comfortable with you when you read this. I had no one with me in that god-awful village in the jungle except Channing, he came rarely since I was better at the job in hand—waiting patiently as usual—than he was. How long it took those two tribes to pull themselves together into one power bloc Channing could then deal with. He must have gotten himself cured—a quick and easy cure, too, as Dr. Clement told me—back at headquarters and simply assumed that he hadn't, after all, infected me. I remember he stayed away for two months, probably to be sure I didn't reinfect him. I never told him when I wasn't feeling well, he hated all that, and the only symptom I had was so mild I'd forgotten it myself until Dr. Pulaski in New York told me I didn't have arthritis at all—after that one visit, the first really thorough check-up I'd had—chest X ray, blood tests, when he helped me track down the likely date so damn long ago—I never went back to him, he knew Channing slightly. I told Pulaski we were going to Switzerland in two days, that I'd have the surgery there. I had other plans, you see. Plans of my own, for once. How like Channing, isn't it, Perce, to have forestalled me from finding out the reason for our never having children—mumps indeed. I laugh now, as he must have secretly laughed at me. I remember him coming into that horrible barn of a house we had to live in at Paul Revere—he was so long-faced, had a magnum of champagne, spent the evening letting me reassure him he hadn't failed me, that our marriage was everything, perfect, children or not. He must have been sweating a bit as he laughed, though, until I assured him I'd cancel my own appointment for fertility tests, which of course I did. How quickly, being Channing, he must have filed the whole episode in the back of his head, to be dealt with later some other way if it ever arose again.

It didn't, I never was one for going for check-ups and so forth, silly now, but after all, I was never ill. Just dying.

Now I'm tired, Perce; to go on living, even if I could, and Clement doesn't deceive me, it's most unlikely I can, would be only a repetition. Beemeadows, which I love, does exist and will go on but I know what the doctors think when they *don't* tell me not to take so many drugs for pain, even though I'm addled by them so often—they won't tell me the disease *hasn't* marched its microscopic steps to my brain; they think they are being very kind. No more Beemeadows for me, not on that basis. I would have let Clement do his best earlier, his nice surgical guillotine, but I had a few ends to tidy up. Suicide by delay, perhaps.

We're leaving tomorrow, Channing for his power perches in Boston and so on, and me for Albany and two days of tests before they operate on Thursday. Two days in bed sound heaven—as close as I shall get to it after what I have done, but Channing always expected me to attend to things; I think I have for once and all for us both.

Love,
Louisa

Please see, Perce, my body is cremated and cleansed for all time. Put my ashes anywhere in the sun—I am so cold.

\*

"Sweet Jesus!" Helen whispered, handing the letter back to Simon. His eyes were wet.

"She killed Channing, you know."

"Yeah. That bowl. Okay, I know I wasn't supposed to, but I peeked—Pandora. My cast slipped and I dropped the bowl to keep from falling. It broke—the damn thing was riddled inside with the cut-off tips of those old poisoned darts. She must have put them all through that piece of clay, they're sharp as hell and would have gone right into his hands when he started to raise the bowl on the wheel. That's what we saw in the morgue, isn't it?"

"Yes. And there's one in the throat of Magnificat."

"What?"

"Louisa must have wanted to be sure the curare on the darts was still effective—it lasts forever, apparently—she had all the darts in the pocket of her smock except the one she'd overlooked that stuck in the top of the highboy. There were none in that little quiver when I hung it for her—upside down, as you pointed out."

"I'd forgotten."

"So had I until I was up there Monday with Thelma. Louisa was carrying Magnificat down from her house when she took me to show me where the blackberries were. How easy—she was euphoric, fuddled, out of herself with drugs, she'd been taking more pills up there on top of the morning's dose—to ram one in Magnificat's throat and toss the cat right into the middle of the thicket. I remember when Ray and I buried her the broken bones, we thought—in the cat's throat—looked like bones, claws, feathers, we thought she'd finally choked on a bird. Louisa—Louisa saw that the curare was still potent. She knew her Channing, knew that no matter *when* she died he'd get back to his potting sooner or later —before or after hearing of her death, it didn't matter. He'd finish that set of bowls. Or start to."

"So that's why he went staggering on across the deck through Webby's tacks. Curare attacks the central nervous system, doesn't it—convulsions and excitement for a second or so, then respiratory paralysis, gasping for air—fainting? The flower boxes—it all fits."

"You're very up on your poisons—yes. I wasn't sure until this morning; night before last before dinner I dug up Magnificat and took her to the medical examiner in Pittsfield the next morning—Connolly, very receptive man to my wild concept. He agreed to test the dart in the cat's mouth for curare and the splinters in Channing's hands, and do a further autopsy if he found anything. Remember he'd been interrupted in the middle of examining Channing by that bus holocaust, he was drowning in bodies and it seemed so certain that Channing had simply died of a fall from the deck anyway. But when he did—I'd arranged for him to call me at Ada's this morning—"

"Thank heaven—you thought Webster'd be back in the office and hanging around by the phone? I shudder at what he'd make of this."

"Quite. In any event, Connolly found enough curare in Channing's body to have killed him twice over if he hadn't fallen first. I doubt Louisa would have cared which it was."

"No, I don't think she would. You'll have to go over and

have a long talk with that doctor, though, Simon. No point in the kind of ghoul's glory this'd produce if the papers ever got it."

"I'll need Perce for that." They looked out the window of the diner; he was sitting on the same bench, a squirrel on the tree trunk behind him deciding to trust the quiet presence of the old man.

"You will indeed. Somehow, though, I think he'll do."

# CHAPTER XI

Channing's burial service at Adaams Park was attended by only the invited cream of representatives from all his past associations, although there were a number of irrefusable wreaths from foreign hospitals, schools, institutions he had seen were funded. Delegates from the United Nations, Mortimer from the Bayard Foundation with Miss Wilber, Izzard from the World Council of Churches, the rector and senior warden of St. Jude's, the presidents of Greenfield and Paul Revere colleges, board members of the Teaparty Trust, governors of Adaams Park itself.

Perceval had decreed a graveside service only in the family plot, no eulogy. The bishop officiated, Simon assisting, and, to everyone's surprise, Webby was thurifer, rehearsed by Simon until the heavy censer the boy carried swung and smoked with proper decorum. The boy looked well at last, although Sally was very cross about the incense. Webby had insisted on being allowed to participate, though. He had had another talk with Simon; the carpet tacks were once and for all relegated to their proper place in the boy's mind: quite a destructive thing to do, but not the cause of Adaams' death. Webby must take it on trust from Simon. He did.

Sally, torn away from Mortimer, who seized Miss Wilber and made a dash for his limousine, asked the unspoken question that was hanging in the air after the service. "Why *isn't* Louisa being buried with him? It's ridiculous, they *must* have wanted to be buried together and I'm sure at Beemeadows." The Haywards' car was waiting among the long black limousines, its back seat packed with cartons, books, typewriter, adding machine, easels. There was scarcely room enough left in a corner for Webby. Perce had made it quite plain that the season at Beemeadows was over for the Haywards, the exterminator was coming tomorrow to fumigate and seal the entire second story, among other things. He had seen cockroaches. Sally had given in; they were going back down to New York from the Park directly the service was over.

"I believe Louisa left instructions for another arrangement for her own burial, Sally." Thelma, in a quiet gray dress, led her away from Perce, who was helping Webby out of the cassock and cotta borrowed from the nearby church. "Perce is, after all, their next of kin for all practical purposes, and I'm sure he's being quite scrupulous about their wishes."

"Well, it seems funny to me, but after all, what does it matter? The main thing is how their deaths are going to affect Beemeadows. Now Webster and I have some ideas—"

"I'm sure you do, Sally." Ray opened the car door for her; Webster was already seated with a road map on his knee. Sally climbed in behind the wheel. "We'll have to get together when I get down to New York sometime, Sally—here's your son, now—in you go." The boy scrambled over his father into a constricted nest next to the calculating machine.

"Well," Sally said, starting the engine, "you know we're interested in buying, particularly their house, it would suit our life-style quite well. I'll call you next week."

The Russells stood arm and arm in the drive. "Poor child." Webby was waving from the back window. "Ray, let's tear out all the telephones at the farm."

"Every single one."

*

"Tragic accident causing death of Channing Adaams—" "Died during surgery for a heart condition—" Helen pasted the two obituaries side by side in the last scrapbook, wondering if they'd all go to Adaams Park to the library there. Very likely; Perce would see to that. Channing had been involved in much history, had seized upon his time and left his mark. Perce's professionalism and sense of fairness would make it possible for him to separate his personal hatred for Channing and put it to one side. Besides, the leather-bound history of those two lives was as much a tribute to Louisa as to Channing; he would see she was included in a rightful place in the long histories of the family.

She handed the closed album to Alf Bemis, sitting beside her on the porch. He put it into the carton he had brought out for her, on top of the others, and sealed the box with tape, after putting in it the carefully folded American flag that had been the pall for Channing's coffin and which Perce had given him at the funeral for safekeeping. He's looking better now, Helen thought, he looks—well. Healed. Simon had been right; Alf's father had died the day after Simon's visit, and whether or not the venom and poison he had spewed out at Simon had eased his passing no one would ever know. But at least Alf was free of attempting futile amends; there was color in his face that suited his shaggy dark brows and grizzling hair.

"How's everything at the log cabin, Alf? Did Katey turn out to be a good tenant?"

"I'll never know if she was or not—Ada and Thelma said they 'went in to be sure the windows were closed' but you know them, they'd never let on if they'd had to scrub the place from top to bottom. She seemed a nice girl this spring, and nothing's missing, so I assume everything was all right. It's great to be back, even if it had been a shambles."

"I know—I never think of myself as having much of a nesting instinct myself, but I always surprise myself at being so darn glad to open the door of my digs on Twelfth Street, dust and junk mail and dead plants and all. Knowing it's there, even when I'm halfway around the world and having a ball, keeps my sanity."

"Yes, I felt that myself this summer; came near to going off my rocker once in a while over there and probably would have if I didn't know deep down I'd get back here sooner or later. Damn stiff-necked pride; should have let my friends help out instead of beating them off with a stick." He stretched out his legs, sat back in his chair. He's a comfortable man to be with, Helen thought, wishing she could ever tell him of the wild possibilities she and Simon had explored about him not so long ago on this very porch. Never, of course.

"I've been thinking a lot about Louisa," he said, clearing his throat. "Perce told me she'd known of her heart condition for some months and delayed and delayed the operation in order to set things in order for Channing—talk about stiff-necked pride; I wish somehow I could have known, known her better. Been able to help. She'd always seemed so powerfully in charge of things, running the show here and all. But I wonder—you and I were talking of a sense of home and what a strength that can be, knowing we have ours. She never did, until these last three years; I wonder what took its place for her."

"Channing, of course. His life. And probably the hope of an eventual Beemeadows. Much more for her than for Channing, from the little I saw of them—the farm seemed to be a perch for him, but certainly not for her. She seemed to have really, finally, come into her own here for the first time. It seems so sad she had so very little of it."

"I know. I think I've been perceiving them backwards, in a way." A late, unexpected firefly flickered in the woods leading up the hill. "Channing's death doesn't seem the—waste I thought it did when I first heard; I think if he'd lived, not had that stupid accident, his life would have been only more of the same. But for Louisa—"

"Yeah, she *was* cut off from a beginning. I see what you mean." They sat comfortably together in the richening gloom of early evening. A week since Channing's funeral, almost two weeks since Louisa's death. Simon and Perce had pulled it off, Helen thought, sipping the mint julep Alf had made and brought out for them. The medical examiner and district attorney had spent a long, open afternoon with the two distant cousins, now so close. Simon was still cursing himself for having opened that Pandora's box of the dead cat and Channing's hands at all, had used every strategy and wile and skill in his considerable arsenal of diplomacy. Perce's frankness about Louisa's illness, the possibility of her mind being affected and the surgeon's written testimony that that was indeed likely, either from disease itself or from too heavy use of pain-relieving drugs, had won the day. The cause of Channing's death was left as accidental. And Louisa had been so demonstrably ill all summer—given her devotion to Channing's priorities; it was fully in character for her to have postponed surgery, and finally have attempted to have it done as quietly and anonymously and with as little trouble to anyone as possible.

"We must all learn to bother each other more, I think." Bemis spoke out suddenly; the dusk, their inability to see each other clearly although they sat side by side, acting as a lubricant to his inner thoughts as much as the julep. Funny, he's been thinking just along my own track, Helen said to herself.

"What d'you say to that, old shoe?" she said to Simon, who had come out and was now sitting on the step, holding her cast in his lap. "I, for one, agree with Alf entirely—we've got to stamp our feet and make our needs known instead of sucking our thumbs."

"I'm for it, Alf. For Beemeadows, particularly; without it I doubt any community could survive."

"Beemeadows not survive?" They heard Perce bustling toward them across the porch, his white apron barely visible in the gloom. "Rubbish. Fine julep, by the way, Alf." He struck the dinner bell thoroughly. "I want everyone here on time tonight; Judah has brought up an extremely welcome token of his esteem for Ada—how he procured it here so far from the sea is a mystery, but we are dining on a striped bass so large I've had to poach it in a ham boiler."

"Amazing thing," Simon laughed, "a real concert-grand-size fish if I've ever seen one. With the head still on, praise be."

"Does that make a difference?" Helen asked, chewing on the mint from her drink.

"I'll let Simon explain—I must see to the sauce. Alf, send up a flare when you see the Russells coming, Judah and Ada are at their wagering in the living room, I can whisk in the yolks when Thelma and Ray—" he muttered happily to himself, pushing through the young evening back into his kitchen, where he busied himself with a bulb baster, pulling off the liquid the resting fish was exuding, as perfectly cooked fish do. Weeping for the joy of their own excellence, I daresay, Perce thought, stopping for a moment as he heard Simon's clear, rich voice begin to sing, unaccompanied except for the firefly twinkling contrapuntally in the woods, then joined shyly but firmly and well by Alf's tenor and a moment later by Judah's harmonica from the living-room doorway: "—and the touch of Sylvia's hand—is as light as morning dew —" Perce began separating eggs as he heard Thelma's alto coming near: "—All that's beautiful and bright, that is Sylvia to the night."

*

"Simon?"

"Yes, love?"

"Thank you for the song. I needed it."

"I know. I too. We all did. Warm enough?"

"If you'll give my other pillow back I will be. It's tomorrow, isn't it? I heard you and Perce after dinner."

"Yes. You needn't, you know—"

"Oh, Christ, Simon, when will you shut up? Of course I needn't—I want to. You are so damn dumb sometimes, especially when you're being your smartest about everything else."

"Looking back, I wasn't so smart about exhuming that pathetic cat; if I'd had the faintest idea about Louisa's condition, her state of mind or health, d'you think I'd ever have stirred up any of that—as it was, I was only interested in how smart I could be, how terribly brilliant—"

"Oh, nonsense, you weren't at all—*trying* to be smart, I mean, you just were. I was as deep in it as you were, remember Katey and me at the Black Griffon? And with good reason. There was something stinking as high as heaven about the fall Channing took. Anybody would have done what we did with the information we had. You can't just leave something like that alone." She lit a cigarette, handed one to Simon in the dark, its tip glowing red. "Poor Louisa, she must have been so single-minded at the end she couldn't conceive beyond paying Channing back for all the years he'd taken from her, both the past and the future, and not thought at all that her booby trap for him could possibly rebound on someone else. Like Webby. You and I have such cynical minds—no, don't deny it, healthily cynical—everybody was reeking with motives for wanting Channing to suffer. Sally wanted his job for Webster, Ada maybe thinking with Channing out of the picture Katey'd leave and she might have another chance with Judah—"

"You never told me that—a bit farfetched?"

"Don't kid yourself, remember Medea? *She* was Greek—well, near enough as makes no matter. And Judah himself, remember how drunk he got that day Channing died? He'd just felt the horns he was wearing, that's enough of a motive right there. And Perce—if Louisa had shown that snapshot of Terry—no, even ill as she was she wouldn't have done that, not deliberately, but he might have seen it by accident and put two and two together—"

"As a matter of fact, he did. Wanted to thrash out his feelings this afternoon; took me up to the meadow and got it all out—no, no, not a confession, a cousinly confidence only, so I can tell you. He hadn't known of Terry's pregnancy until she died, although he'd managed to put some very useful slip-covers on his awareness of her habits while she was alive and never really took them off until this month when he did find the snapshot by accident. The hatred for Channing on top of his lifelong jealousy of all that flair and brilliance and success, especially when he compared it to the superficial drabness of his own life, was terrifying to listen to. But the burden of it all was his intention this afternoon of some sort of absurd self-imposed penance for all those feelings. Talked him out of that in jig-time, but it took some doing."

"What sort of penance?"

"Puritan Roundhead balderdash—seems the Teaparty Trust has sounded him out about taking Channing's post; of course it's the one thing Channing had that Perce was equal to, if not better, and he's wanted it all along. Was going to turn it down. I almost murdered him—well, he finally came round. He'll be wonderful at it, best thing in the world for him."

"That's great—just think, on top of all the Teaparty politicking he'll get to do, he'll have to go to Boston once a month and Beemeadows can have fish!"

"Just for that, Miss B., I'll take away your other pillow."

"Aha! Only, my love, if I get to come with it."

\*

They reached the top of the meadow, Helen's back hot in the afternoon sun, and quietly greeted the waiting group. Ray had pried open the hideous funeral urn the undertaker had delivered, and mixed Louisa's ashes in a vast Canton-ware bowl Thelma had filled with blossoms and blossoms of Louisa's white roses, and green leaves stripped from the thorny branches. It was sitting on a large boulder, Perce, bare-headed, standing next to it, his hand on the rock.

Simon pulled a stole from his pocket, kissed it, placed it around his neck, and opened a small Book of Common Prayer, much worn and with the *Louisa Anstruther* stamped on the cover in gold almost entirely rubbed away. He nodded at Perce, who picked up the bowl steadily.

"I am the resurrection and the life—though this body be destroyed, yet shall I see God—and not as a stranger—"

Helen wondered why the tears blinding her eyes and refusing to fall should keep her from hearing Simon's strong baritone except in odd passages. So quiet here, only a tiny whiff of a breeze.

"—the sun shall not burn thee by day, neither the moon by night—preserve thy going out, and thy coming in from this time forth forevermore—"

Judah's face was awash with tears, Ray and Thelma too. Ada and Bemis stepped forward, to stand on either side of Perce as he moved toward Simon.

"Out of the deep I have called unto thee, O Lord—for there is mercy with thee—wherefore my heart is glad—my flesh also shall rest in hope—evermore."

\*

Simon made the sign of the cross over the bowl; Perce moved forward down the fertile sun-drenched green meadow that would now be forever Louisa's, and as they followed him Helen could finally hear Simon.

*

"Unto Almighty God we commend the soul of our sister Louisa, departed, and we commit her body to the ground; earth to earth, ashes to ashes, dust to dust, in sure and certain hope of the resurrection—"

The roses and ashes, lifted by a small late breeze, flew upward for a moment as Perce scattered them from the bowl, then sank forever on either side of the path as they walked down the meadow.

# EPILOGUE

Helen had decided to give in after all; she looked at the cast on her leg stretched out on the bench of the car ferry, halfway across Lake Champlain. Stickers for Sturbridge Village, Bennington Stoneware, the Barre Granite Monument Quarry, Vermont Maple Syrup, Big Bromley—that was a bit of a cheat, no snow and the sticker was cloth and had to be glued on—and Simon was mooching about the ferry, looking for a souvenir shop with something from the ship to add to the collection. The car already had several bumper stickers firmly wired to the fender, but that didn't count. He'd promised her, though, they'd come back down the west side of the lake to Fort Ticonderoga itself; it'd be bound to have all sorts of doodads.

Peaceful, ferry boats. A nice state of suspended animation. Poor old Simon had had to do all the driving, of course, but they were both unexpectedly—diminished, that was it, more than tired this past week of leisurely touring. Funny how little we've talked, and yet how much together we are.

"Sorry, love, this is the best I could do—thought we could perhaps jury-rig it alongside with a bit of tape?" Simon stood in front of her, leaning against the rail, holding a long pencil with a blue felt banner with S.S. *Ticonderoga* in silver glitter stapled to the top, a quizzical look on his face.

"Hmm. It has possibilities. Not too touristy or vulgar, though? I don't want to embarrass you."

"Oh, it's definitely very chic, very. If you're going to do a thing, do it all the way—I vote yes. A bit of the glitter may rub off in bed; perhaps we'd better strike the colors at night and raise them fresh every morning?"

"Good idea. Here, I'll just tuck it down inside until we get to a tape store. How about a hot dog?"

"Dear lord, woman, after all those pancakes at breakfast?"

"I know, but I want the full rich experience and ferry boats and hot dogs go hand in hand. Don't be mean." Vermont was fading behind him into mist and distance, the urban outline of Burlington already invisible. "Mustard, relish, and sauerkraut, please."

"Yassm." He brought back the hot dogs, they sat munching peacefully in the shade, the early morning sun beginning to burn away a bit of mist that still lingered. Helen pulled the road atlas out of her hold-all, opened it to a map of the area.

"Now when we land, there's a place called Au Sable Chasm that's bound to be worth a detour—I can see it now, black-top parking lots, souvenir shops galore with everything from fuzz-ball key rings to blown-glass animals and pennies in little bottles—it's a must, don't you think?"

"Absolutely. Awsable, is it?"

"Au Sable, but only between you and me and not out loud while we're there, for heaven's sakes."

"Sorry, I'll remember." He stretched out his long legs on the deck, folded his arms and closed his eyes. "I'm thinking of making a major investment, Helen."

"Yeah?"

"A raccoon tail for the radio antenna—we're a bit short of space on the bumpers already."

"I don't know, Simon—maybe. I'll tell you what, I'm for it if it's dyed green. Natural's out this year."

She stuffed the road atlas back into her bag, pulled out an envelope. "Oh, my God, this was down at the bottom—Ada gave it to me as we were leaving last week—" She opened it, pulled out a piece of paper, two checks paper-clipped to the top.

Dear kids,

What do you know, you both won at Aqueduct last week! Know you'll see how it skipped my mind until now. Nephew sent the weekly winnings today and maybe it'll be more fun for you to open this and celebrate down the road apiece—may take some of the bluer memories away from Beemeadows for you; hope so, we all want you back anytime. Helen, you put ten on ※9 in the ninth—Proud Wastrel paid four to one so here's your forty bucks. And Simon's Irresolute shouldn't of had but did leave them all at the post in the eighth; sixty to you, Father. What's your system, anyway? Don't forget the action moves over to Saratoga in August if you're going to be down that way. Judah's got his hand back in, now he's ahead over three thousand—can't seem to keep my mind on blackjack now he's around again. Keep in touch.

Love,<br>Ada.

"Proud Wastrel," Helen laughed, waving the check. "And I didn't even know the name of the nag. Appropriate, though."

"How so?"

"Nine in the ninth—nine letters in Simon Bede, that's what I bet on—arcane, but profitable. I suspect the Proud Wastrel's *me*."

"If so, then Irresolute applies to me—"

He picked up Helen's hand lightly; she gave it a squeeze. "Helen—"

"Nope, you're wrong. I know. Eight letters. Resolute!"